Other titles in this series:

Who knew second chances could get better—and hotter—after midnight?

Even special operatives make mistakes. Roades Knight knows *that* better than anyone. As punishment for the mission he muddled up, he's officially off duty. But his dreams of quiet time spent fishing vanish when he gets a frantic call from his ex.

No matter what, he *will* help her. And this time, he *won't* let her down.

Carissa's island home is a disaster. Literally. Hurricane Maria left nothing but turmoil in her wake. Supplies are limited, and gangs of tyrants are stealing from the people who them most. Among the thieves? Her own brother. She knows Roades can get through to him. What she *doesn't* know if she can stop herself for falling for the hardened operative—*again.*

Can Roades and Carissa find their happily ever after somewhere between keeping her brother out of trouble and helping rebuild a ravaged land?

After MidKnight

by

Em Petrova

Chapter One

Roades had just completely and catastrophically ended his career. One fucking misstep had almost blown up the whole mission in the faces of the elite Knight Ops team. If not for his teammates, all would have been lost, and thank God they'd pulled it out of their asses at the last minute.

But Roades' head was still on the chopping block, and Colonel Jackson had a cleaver in his hand.

Okay, it was just a file but if it was Roades', then it was thick from other times he went off the rails and took matters into his own hands. He wasn't some young pup anymore, and he knew how to follow orders. What had gotten him in trouble was following his gut too, and that might mean the end of his career in the special forces.

The thump of Colonel Jackson's boots as he paced the room in front of Roades was a constant drum in his chest. He held the salute for one minute... two. His arm was beginning to ache, and Jackson knew it. Still, the colonel wasn't going to give that *at ease* anytime soon. Not when he was fuming and the man to take it out on was Roades.

His biceps started to burn but he'd experienced worse. He held the pose and counted each step the colonel took. He was up to two hundred twelve when Jackson jerked around to face him.

The colonel's stare was direct and piercing. If Roades was a lesser man or even a couple years younger, he might piss his pants. But he was a Knight—and Knights didn't tuck tail and run.

Jackson waved the file in Roades' face, the breeze off it smelling papery and cooling the sweat on his brow. "At ease, you little piss-ant."

Roades dropped into a less formal pose, his muscles thanking him. He dragged in a deep breath and waited for the ass-chewing he was about to receive and then some.

"You realize what you've jeopardized for our division, Knight?"

Yeah, he'd gone in with guns blazing, his sights set on the target… that apparently wasn't the target at all but one of their own undercovers. An agent who'd been working the enemy for nearly a year, easing into a position of trust and regard.

But looking down the barrel of Roades' weapon had made the undercover talk.

Loudly.

"Sir, all due respect but—"

Jackson whirled on him. "You know, every time I hear all due respect from one of you Knight boys' mouths, my teeth just about break off from grinding them. If you respected anything, you would not be in this position right this minute."

"Understood, Colonel, but—"

Colonel Jackson took off pacing again. "But bullshit. You got the wrong mark and therefore the undercover was made."

"There was nothing to tell me an undercover was even on site, sir."

"You knew how sensitive this mission was and you fucked it up."

"I did not fuck it up, sir. We pulled through. The captures were made, the victims recovered and safe." Roades was grinding his own teeth now. Goddamn, he hated being told off, and being youngest of the five brothers, he had a lot of experience at it. Didn't mean he stomached it for long, and he'd been well-trained to be mouthy.

When Jackson stared him down, his eyes were bloodshot, and a vein throbbed in his temple. "Damn, son, you just don't get it, do you? That undercover is now a target of that group, and he cannot go back into service without taking extreme measures. He's lost a year of work finding the man responsible for this crime, was closer to the target than anyone ever has been since the inception of the terrorist group. And you walk in there and pull a gun on him."

"Sir, it isn't my fault he squawked like a parrot, sir."

Jackson stepped up, face in Roades' face. "Are you blaming him, Knight?"

He steeled his spine. "An agent should be prepared to take a bullet if necessary, sir. He wasn't. He collapsed under the pressure, and that is not my fault, sir."

"Jeezus, Knight," Jackson drawled in his Southern Louisiana twang that didn't always come through in orders. "You *are* dumping the blame on the agent. When it was *you* who acted irresponsibly by pulling your weapon in the first place! Were you ordered to pull your weapon?"

Roades didn't even wince in the face of his superior's shouting, nor did he answer the question the colonel already knew. His chest burned with the need to yell back, but this wasn't his commander and big brother Ben. His brother might kick his ass but Jackson could — and most likely would — end his career in the special ops force.

"Sir, I saw my opportunity and I took it. Back in 2011, if that SEAL hadn't seen Bin Laden and taken the chance, we'd still be — "

Jackson jabbed a finger at Roades' face, an inch from his nose. "Not another word, Knight!"

His chest rose and fell with the effort not to spew it back at the colonel. He kept telling himself it was in his best interest to be still and await the punishment he was sure to receive.

Jackson flipped open the file and read a bit on whatever page was on top. His brow creased and he slammed the file shut again. "This is full of your misdemeanors, Knight." He started reciting some, and Roades tuned them all out. Each he'd gotten flack from or even a slap on the wrist, but he wouldn't be so lucky this time.

"What the hell am I going to do with you?" Jackson seemed to speak to himself rather than Roades, so he remained silent.

He could almost hear his brothers chiding him with a *silent for once*. But Roades pushed his brothers from his mind and gazed at the colonel.

"Three months." He held up three fingers, the last three, his thumb and forefinger creating a ring. "Three months off. Your team will receive a replacement until you're off probation."

"Three—"

"Do you want to make it six?"

He gulped down the words he was about to say and stood straight and silent.

Jackson resumed his pacing. "See yourself out, Knight."

He saluted, throat clamped shut on all the crap he'd like to say in retaliation. But he walked out of the building and straight to his bike. The Ninja had earned him his nickname on the team—a name he wouldn't hear for three months.

"Dammit to hell," he muttered and swung his leg over the seat. His team would all still be debriefing, and he didn't know what the hell to do with himself. Three months of being left out of missions, unable to stand up next to his brothers and their teammate Rocko and protect his country.

He ran his fingers through his hair. He'd really fucked up.

Sure, he'd see everyone, but they would be unable to include him in anything classified. And just what the hell was he supposed to do for three months?

He kicked the bike into gear and sped out of the parking lot, ripping between two cars and causing one to lay on his horn. The bike leaned, but Roades was as good as a stunt driver and he whipped it upright to take a turn at high speed.

Reckless, his family would call him, and what the hell did he care right now? He didn't.

He gassed it, and the lightweight bike pulled a wheelie. He rode it out for several city blocks before setting it down. Open road—that's what he needed right now.

With his fists clamped on the grips and his throat burning with a bellow of frustration and fury, he gunned the bike, making his escape from reality for however long he could.

* * * * *

The empty water jug thumped against Carissa's hip as she made her way through the town. The aid station was set up in the town square and every Monday and Thursday they could collect water and supplies. She'd been out of water for longer than she cared to think about it, but she didn't feel bad for sharing what she had with her neighbor.

Mr. Báez waved at her, angling across the street to reach her side.

"How are you today?" she asked, noting the sheen of perspiration coating his skin and the brightness in his eyes. He was fevered.

"Fine today. Feeling much better."

She pursed her lips. As a nurse, she'd say otherwise. Mr. Báez had been battling an infection in his lungs for a while now, and she couldn't convince the stubborn older man to take the antibiotics she could offer.

He struggled to shift the water container he carried to the other hand, and she gasped at the sight of his red, swollen skin. She dropped her water can and it clattered into the street to lie there with the debris.

Carissa grabbed Mr. Baez's elbow to draw him near enough to examine his swollen hand and forearm. Her gaze snapped up and she stared into his dark chocolate eyes. "When did you cut yourself?"

"Last week sometime."

"Clearing the debris from your yard?" Hurricane Maria had sat over their island for days, slamming them, picking up items, twisting them and dropping them again. Her own yard was still a wreck, but that was because she was too busy helping others to clean it up.

"*Si*, from my yard."

She turned his hand over and saw the source of the fever in its full, angry, purplish-red glory. She tracked the redness up his arm. "You're lucky — this isn't yet blood poisoning. But if you don't get to my clinic today it will be soon. I'll need to clean the infection out."

"I'm sure it will hurt too," he said with a mocking tone.

"Of course it will. If you'd come to me after you cut it, you would be healed by now. Now your body is battling two infections." She released her hold on his arm and picked up both their cans. "Get to my clinic right now and wait for me while I fetch our water."

Before the older man could retaliate, she hurried away with the water cans. Cursing under her breath at stubborn old men who were stuck in their ways and again at the devastation of their island. She cursed their lack of aid so much that it was a constant mantra in her mind.

The clinic where she'd worked had been closed, and she had set up a makeshift clinic in the shed behind her house to treat patients. The townsfolk came to her for everything from coughs to broken bones. She did what she could, but despite it being prohibited for medical personnel to leave Puerto Rico, many of the doctors had fled to the mainland and her resources were limited. All her first-aid supplies and medicines came from…

Well, the supplies weren't easy to come by.

She reached the town square where workers were siphoning fresh water from a tank into their containers. The line was long and she had plenty of time to look around. Nothing had changed in town from the previous time she was here — the streets still littered with debris and shops were blackened shells with the windows blown in. No lights lit a single corner. They were without power.

In the line ahead, shouting broke out. She moved to see what was going on. The Spanish came in spurts of anger, and it took her a minute to understand. Then it hit her.

They said they had no more water.

"What's happening?" she asked the person ahead of her, but the woman just shook her head, looking as confused as Carissa.

Louder shouts this time and one of the men doling out the water got shoved.

Carissa started forward, but the woman in front of her jabbed an elbow at her. "Get out of here before you're caught in the fight!"

Carissa darted a look at the head of the line. People threw punches and others fell to the ground. No water was flowing, and her stunned mind drank it all in, along with the words floating back to her.

No water. It's all they could get that you won't need to pay for.

Pay for?

"Go!" the woman in front of her yelled in her face. "If you get hurt, who will treat us?"

All hell was breaking loose, and the mob of people in need of clean, safe water were rioting against those who didn't have enough.

But why wasn't there enough? Who was asking them to pay?

She scooped up her water jugs and ran for it. After she broke free of the crowd, she glanced over her shoulder, saw the turmoil and kept running.

At the next block, she stopped and turned to stare again. Police were involved, what few were in their area after the disaster, and they were rounding people up.

Carissa looked down at the empty jugs in her hands. What now?

She had to find somebody who had fresh water. Until they cleaned up from the hurricane, the only way to get the things they needed was through the black market, an underground supply chain that mostly came from looters out for profit.

But the idea of water being one of those commodities made her stomach twist.

Getting out of Puerto Rico was not an option for her—she had to stay and help. This was her motherland, her people.

She shook her long, dark hair out of her eyes and headed east in the town. The walking was laborious and her throat was parched. She had to keep going, though, for Mr. Báez who would definitely need his portion of water to combat his fever.

He was in her clinic waiting for her now.

When she walked up an alley and knocked at a door, she heard people talking within the building. She knocked again, and the door swung open enough for a man to poke his head out.

"Angel, let me in."

The handsome man with a fresh, red cut on his face saw her and opened the door, allowing her to pass. The building was dark, lit only by what candles and oil lanterns they had on hand. In the middle of the room was a huge table and on the surface were supplies ranging from matches to handguns and even candy bars.

Her mouth watered at the thought of chocolate, but she needed a drink more.

Music played and, in another room, somebody was singing along with the Latin rhythm.

"What do you need, Carissa?" Angel wasn't a man to cross, and the only reason he tolerated her was because she'd insisted on stitching him after he'd been in a knife fight alongside her brother.

She looked around for her brother Hernan but if he was here, she didn't see him. She faced Angel again. "Water. They're saying the water has been held from us and we must pay for it. Is that true?"

His eyebrow twitched upward, as did the corner of his mouth. "You know you can get water anytime you want it."

Confusion drew her own brows together. "How?"

"The prince of Puerto Rico has figured out a way to earn money on everything that comes in, and now he's controlling the water."

"I don't understand." She shook her head. "Who is the prince? What does that even mean? Is it a gang?"

Angel folded his arms, legs braced wide. "You could say that."

Anger bubbled inside Carissa. "These people need clean, safe water and this person is stopping it from reaching us unless we pay him?"

"Sounds like it."

She was small and against violence, but right now she needed to give this 'prince' a piece of her mind. "Where is he? Is he here?"

"Your brother isn't here today. He's out on the docks."

Her spine snapped with her jerk of shock. "My brother," she said faintly, putting two and two together and coming up with a terrible sum. Hernan was involved in this treacherous scheme. She met Angel's eyes. "He's really back to his old ways, isn't he?"

She wanted to believe that knife fight was it. And the looting was bad enough. Now this was a crime against humanity.

Years before, her little brother had been young and hard-headed enough to believe he could live a life of crime and not get caught. After several tussles with the law, one person had talked sense into him and he'd stopped.

For a time.

Or maybe he'd only fooled her into believing he'd stopped.

But no, Roades Knight had a power over Hernan unlike any other. He was father figure and big brother rolled into one, and after spending time with him, Hernan had straightened up, finished school and gotten a job.

That was before the hurricane, and now there were no jobs. At least not ones on the up and up.

She swallowed the aching lump in her throat at the idea of her little brother lording his power over the land, keeping people like Mr. Báez from even a glass of water to drink.

She stepped toward Angel. "Please tell me where to find him."

"Can't." He twisted from her imploring gaze. "But there's water here, and you can take what you need. If you can't carry it all, take the cart and we'll come by and get it."

Dragging in a deep breath, she racked her brain for a way out of taking anything from Angel and his looters. But she'd been using him for a week now to supply her clinic and get medicines her patients wouldn't have any other way.

She raised her chin a notch, meeting his dark eyes. "I need medicines too."

He waved a hand at the table. "You'll find them there. I said take what you need."

At what cost?

She'd have to pay the price later. Right now, she didn't have a choice—her hands were bound and it was either do this deal or let her people down.

Setting down her water jugs, she stepped up to the table, opened her cloth bag slung across her body and began filling it. Each item she took came with a steep price, and it wasn't one she wanted to pay. It was for the greater good, though.

Once she had all she needed, she started for the water. Angel caught her arm, his presence intimidating even though she'd known him when he was half her size.

"We'll come by and get that crate from you later."

The crates of painkillers had been her only bargaining power. Given to her by the doctor she'd worked closely with in the clinic, who had also fled to the mainland. He'd left her with the crates, and she'd never realized that she sat on a goldmine.

Angel would sell the drugs on the black market and in return, she'd get medications for heart disease, blood pressure and other life-saving drugs for anyone who came to her for help.

What made her any different from Hernan? She was still engaged in illegal activity.

She pulled away from Angel's grasp and walked stiffly into the next room. Hundreds of water jugs sat there and so did the cart he'd mentioned, a two-handled wooden box on wheels. She could easily take a dozen jugs if she could move the heavy weight.

And she would do her best.

Damn you, Hernan. The minute she set eyes on her little brother, she'd give him a piece of her mind right before she slapped him silly.

Chapter Two

Roades walked into the garage with two fishing rods and a tacklebox, heading for the corner where his mother insisted they all keep their sporting goods. Leaning against the wall were more than a dozen rod-and-reel combos as well as a dinky pole from when Chaz decided to head north one winter and do some ice fishin'. Needless to say, it hadn't been touched in a while.

After setting everything in the corner, he turned to go inside and there sat the weight set one of his brothers had received as a Christmas present one year. As a Marine, he kept fit doing hundreds of pushups per night but he hadn't lifted in a while. Maybe he would after grabbing a drink.

When he stepped inside the mudroom, he found a rifle leaned in the corner. "Hey, *Maman,* is Chaz going to the range to shoot?"

His mother's head popped around the refrigerator door. "How would I know? You boys have been leaving your weapons in my kitchen for so many years that I don't even notice them anymore."

He chuckled and came forward to take the head of lettuce from her hand. "You told us off about it more times than I can count."

"Yeah, gave that up too. Don't care to waste my breath. Here, take this too." She passed him a small bag of tomatoes.

"Salad for dinner tonight?" He dropped an impromptu kiss to her cheek.

Her eyes widened with surprise but she nodded. "What was that for?"

"Just felt like it. Can't a son show his *maman* he appreciates her?"

"You only appreciate me so much because you've been hanging around the house eating for weeks." She closed the fridge door, a pepper and a cucumber in hand.

Yeah, he was bored as fuck too. Since being put on probation, he'd fished out every body of water in the area. He'd spent hours at the gun range. And he'd tried warming a barstool but that had gotten annoying fast.

"What's for dinner besides salad?" he asked.

"Chicken and baked potatoes. I still have to run to the market for chicken, though."

"I'll drive you. Are you ready to go now?"

She eyed him but finally nodded. "Give me a minute to tidy myself." She went into the bathroom and Roades leaned against the counter, tapping his boot on the hardwood floor. The house was silent—

17

where was his sister? His only brother who wasn't married was Chaz and he was on a mission.

Where? Roades could only imagine the fun the Knight Ops team was having without him.

"Ready." His mother breezed past him to the door. In the driveway, he pointed to his bike. "Want to ride the Ninja?"

"No, I do not want to ride the Ninja!" She flushed as she realized how that sounded, and Roades laughed. She was used to her boys' foul senses of humor and fouler mouths, but they could still get her blushing sometimes. Their youngest sister Lexi was the easier target, though.

He held the door of his beat-up truck for her. She looked in at the Coke cans on the floor.

"Sorry." He gathered the cans and tossed them into the bin in the garage before getting behind the wheel. The drive was short, and his mind was with his team. Then he realized his mother was talking about his other sister.

Glancing over, he said, "You heard from Tyleri?" Lexi's twin hated having a boy's name, so he and his brothers had stuck an I on the end to appease her. Which only ticked her off more.

"Yes, she's got leave at the end of the month and we'll have a big dinner. If your brothers are home, that is."

Ouch. That stung to think that he'd be here and not his brothers. Off being heroes without him.

The grocery store didn't remotely lift his spirits but he pushed the cart for his *maman* as she shopped.

"Roades."

Her serious tone had him looking at her. "What is it?"

"You like this?"

"Like what?"

"Grocery shopping with your *maman*."

"Yeah, it's great." He reached out to a shelf and plucked off a random box, holding it up.

She eyed the tampons in his hand. "You sure about that?"

He grunted and put the tampons back. They continued to stroll and he pushed the cart with the squeaky wheel.

"I don't think you're enjoying yourself one bit," she went on.

"It's a vacation. I've been hard at it since I joined up at eighteen."

She placed some grits in the cart and continued down the aisle. "You won't convince me this is how you want to spend your time. Playing chauffeur to me and fishin' or shootin'."

"Well, I was going to lift some weights later," he began.

She pierced him in her stare and he stopped moving, feeling ten again. When *Maman* gave them that look, they knew they'd better zip their traps and open their ears.

"You're not happy, Roades, and you've got two more months of probation. Maybe it's time to find something to do that isn't focused on yourself."

He recoiled. "I'm helping around the house as much as I can. There isn't much to do."

She gave a shake of her head, which set the bun on her nape wobbling. "That isn't what I mean, son."

"What do you think I should be doing instead?"

When she looked at him, her expression softened. "You're smart—you'll find something."

After carrying her bags to the truck and stowing them in the back, he drove home in silence. His mind focused on what she'd said but damn if he could think of anything worth filling his time with. Charities weren't him. He was more of a save-the-day type, and those jobs were scarce on the ground.

* * * * *

Carissa raked her fingers through her freshly-washed hair. It felt good to be clean and have enough to drink, but the price of the water turned her stomach. To discover it was her own brother hoarding the supply...

She heard the key in the lock and looked up as her cousin Mari entered the small house they shared. After her parents' car accident when she was studying nursing, she'd had to work full-time to keep the house just to give her brother a home. Mari, being five years older, was able to move in and help. They'd saved the house but not her brother, it seemed.

If only Roades had remained in her life. Even at the young age of seventeen, he'd been the strong male authority figure that their father hadn't had the heart to be.

"You look moody, as usual," Mari said, setting down her purse.

Carissa stifled a groan. Her cousin regularly told her to lighten up, but the weight hadn't lifted from Carissa in far too many years. Her life felt like a series of responsibilities, and at times the weight grew too heavy to bear. Sometimes, she wished she could just sit and stare at the ocean and let her mind go blank.

She dropped her head against the couch cushion and stared at the ceiling instead. There was a water spot where the roof had leaked after the hurricane. Another responsibility.

She tore her gaze away and fixed it on her cousin. "Have you seen Hernan lately?"

Mari arched a brow and drifted to the couch. She sank next to Carissa and pulled the elastic band from her hair, letting the brown locks drift to her shoulders.

"I don't like the way you asked that, Carissa. What's going on with Hernan?"

A lump of anger and disappointment lodged in her throat. "He's the reason nobody has water."

"What?"

"Yes, he's cut off the supply and you can only get it for a price. It's... It's horrible!"

"But he gave us some water?" Mari looked over Carissa's wet hair.

"No, I used the rainwater from the barrel," she muttered. No way would she wash her hair with something so dear as the fresh water.

The concern didn't leave Mari's face. "You're certain Hernan is responsible?"

Mari didn't know of the agreement between her and Angel. If she did, she would not keep her disapproval to herself. She'd always believed Hernan's friend was trouble – and she was right.

Carissa nodded. "I'm sure of it. The *pequeno mierda* needs put in his place. Who can do that, though? Not you or me."

Her cousin didn't even blink at her calling her brother a little shit. "The police?"

Her little brother had been in trouble with the law before, and Roades had come into her life at that time and set him straight. The idea of giving up her brother to the police burned. There had to be another way.

Yeah, Roades.

No. The man had been out of her life for five years. At one time, he would have done anything for her, gone to any lengths to make her happy. She'd met him in New Orleans while visiting a relative, and

22

he'd swept her off her girlish feet. After spending a month falling in love with him, her time in Louisiana was up, and she returned to Puerto Rico.

That was when he showed up at her door bearing a ring with a proposal on his lips. With so much love pouring out of her, she'd jumped into his arms and said yes. Her parents had welcomed him to the family and he'd stayed with them while her mother and aunts planned their wedding ceremony.

But on the morning she was to wed Roades, she woke to a thundering knock on their door. Her father had handled Mr. Knight in his calm, passive way, agreeing they were very young to marry. The words had sliced through Carissa, and Roades had thrown her a serious look before going outside with his father.

After agonizing minutes, Roades had come back inside and taken Carissa by the hand. She hardly remembered the words he'd spoken—just the meaning.

He was breaking it off. Leaving her. He promised to call and write but in the end, he'd done neither. Over the course of months and years, she'd realized he was gone from her life. And to allow his family to split their bond… Well, he must not have really loved her in the first place.

Now she looked at the whole situation as a blessing. They'd both been too young to know what they wanted out of life let alone a marriage. It would have only ended badly.

But Roades was still often on her mind, especially today since learning what Hernan was doing.

"Well, what else can we do?" Mari was asking.

She shook her head, that weight of helplessness—hopelessness—settling over her once more. "I'll think of something." She turned a smile she didn't feel on her cousin. "I left you enough rainwater to wash your hair too. Let's hope it rains this week."

Her cousin returned her smile and smacked at Carissa. "Of course it's going to rain this week. How long have you lived here, Carissa?"

If she'd married Roades, she probably would have moved to Louisiana with him. By now—

She cut off the thought. Roades wasn't for her anymore—that ship had long sailed. But if he could stop Hernan from the crime he was committing...

She waited until Mari was in the bathroom and she heard water sloshing into the sink. Then she grabbed her cell phone.

Service on the island was spotty since the hurricane. She didn't even know if she could get a call out to Roades or if she had the right number for him anymore.

But thinking of all those poor people standing in line waiting for water they'd never receive gave her no choice.

With shaking hands, she dialed Roades.

24

The number was emblazoned on her brain, and she'd sooner forget her own birthday than how to reach him. It rang once, twice.

Heart thumping, she waited, wondering who would answer. Would it be one of his sisters? She liked them both, each as sassy and full of mischief as the other. Of course, they'd been young teens then. Now they were grown women.

"Knights." The harsh answer about gave Carissa a heart attack. She slapped her hand over her chest.

"R-Roades?"

"Who's this?"

The line crackled.

"You're cutting out. Is this… Is this Carissa?"

Emotion she shouldn't still feel slammed her. She felt herself nod but no words emerged.

Then the line went dead.

She whipped up the phone to call back. Desperation hit, and it had nothing to do with Hernan—it was her bone-deep need to hear Roades' voice again.

She couldn't get out the second call or the third. She tried again half an hour later, but it was the same.

She had no way of reaching him.

Going outside in the dark wasn't always safe, according to Mari, but she didn't care right now. The house felt claustrophobic and she couldn't even draw a full breath. It didn't help that her mind was thick with memories of Roades here on the island with her.

The front stoop was only big enough for one person to sit. She sank to the cracked concrete and looked out across the neighbors' back yards. But she didn't see grass or even weeds—she saw her own wedding bouquet. Her dress, a long confection of light silk with beading outlining the bodice. When she'd tried it on, she'd only thought of how Roades wouldn't be able to keep his hands off her.

She pushed out a sigh. They'd been young and stupid. It was probably for the better that she hadn't reached him by phone because she couldn't face the disappointment of rejection. When he told her he couldn't just fly to Puerto Rico and give her brother hell, she would feel the same stone in her stomach she'd felt on the day Roades' father had shown up at their door.

A figure came through the darkness, and she leaped to her feet. "Who's there?"

"Just me, Carissa. Juanita."

"Oh dear. Is your heart troubling you again?" She rushed off the step, her bare feet on the cool grass as she crossed to the woman who wore a head wrap and a housedress. She grasped the woman's elbow and led her around the back of the house to the small shed that was her clinic.

She turned on the battery-powered light and the space lit with a faint glow. It was enough for Carissa to note her neighbor's paleness, though.

She sat her down and checked her pulse. Rapid and faint, just as she expected.

Concern creased her face as she looked into Juanita's eyes. "Juanita, are you sure you won't go to your daughter in Florida? You need a cardiologist."

She waved a hand. "That life is too fast for an old woman like me. Don't you have any more of those pills you gave me last time? They fixed me up for a spell."

Looking at the locked case where she kept everything from anti-diarrheal pills to the digoxin Juanita spoke of, Carissa wondered for the millionth time how terrible she'd feel if her care backfired. She was not, after all, a doctor. Her training brushed the mere surface of medicine.

But what choice did she have? If she didn't treat Juanita and she died, she'd never forgive herself.

She patted the woman's bony shoulder. "I will give you the pill tonight, Juanita. But I want you to give serious thought to at least visiting your daughter and seeing a cardiologist. What I'm giving you might make you feel better for now, but we both know there's more going on in here." She tapped a forefinger to Juanita's chest.

The older woman sighed. "I'll think on it. You care too much, you know that, don't you? Your *mami* would be proud to see you now."

Yes, her grandmother would have been very proud, had she lived to see Carissa become educated.

And her mother as well, had her life not ended abruptly in the car accident. At least her parents were together. What did Carissa have?

Now she was just feeling sorry for herself, when it was Juanita she should be thinking of.

She gave her some clean water and one of the pills. As the woman swallowed both, Carissa urged her to lie down for a while and she'd monitor her for the night. She got her a lightweight blanket and settled her onto the cot. Then Carissa sat next to her, watching her breathe.

And thinking of the man who'd answered the phone.

* * * * *

Roades hit redial on the phone for the tenth time. When the line remained dead, not even connecting, he slammed the side of his fist off the countertop. "Dammit!"

It was Carissa's number. He'd recognize it if he was blind and had Alzheimer's. The woman was calling him after all this time and that could only mean one thing.

She needed him.

But he couldn't just hop a flight and show up at her door. Hell, he didn't know if she still even lived in the same house. By now, she probably had her own place. She could be married and have a couple kids by now.

A deep ache took over his chest, and he pressed his lips into a firm line. It didn't matter what her marital status was—she'd called for a reason.

It couldn't be accidental. She'd spoken his name.

And damn if the breathy tone of her voice wasn't still sending his libido electrical shock after electrical shock.

"Shit." He'd gone through every cuss word there was between her dropped call and now. He picked up the phone. He was going to try once more and then…

What?

He'd decide in a minute.

He dialed. It remained dead.

"Fucking hell." He set down the receiver again and braced his hands on the counter, breathing hard. His mind flying through the options. Which didn't take long, because he was Knight Ops and they were trained to make decisions in a split second.

Shoving off the counter, he strode out of the kitchen. The house was silent, his parents long since in bed and Lexi was… Well, she was Lexi. She might have sneaked out to run wild with some guy who was inevitably bad for her, for all he knew. Though last he'd heard, she was talking to his own teammate Rocko. And the man had better not fuck with his baby sister or he'd be eating all ten of Roades' knuckles for breakfast, lunch, dinner and a midnight snack.

He reached his room and yanked his duffel out from under the bed. He tossed it on the mattress and started filling it. Weapons and ammo came first and then he piled clothes on top.

After zipping it shut—the whole operation had taken him less than two minutes to complete—he stood there thinking. He needed transport, and no way was he heading out on a domestic flight.

He grabbed his cell and called his friend, a military helicopter pilot who had his own private plane. In his spare time, Cohen threw darts at a map to decide where to fly today. Well, Roades was here to tell him it was Puerto Rico.

"Damn, Roades, it's late." His buddy's voice came to him through the phone.

"Hope you're awake."

"I am. You wanna hit a bar or something? I haven't done the pub crawl in months."

"Nope. I need transport."

A beat of silence. "What trouble are you in?"

"No trouble."

"I heard you—"

"I don't care what you heard. This has nothing to do with OFFSUS."

"If you're AWOL, I won't be involved with aiding a criminal."

That made Roades laugh, a harsh bark that reflected the turmoil inside him right now. Carissa needed him, he felt it deep in his gut. And he was over five hours away from her by air.

"They want me out of their hair for a bit, and I have something to do."

"Can't it wait till morning?"

"No. Cohen, you know you owe me one."

"You're right, I do. But I never thought you'd collect on that favor."

"What good is a fucking favor if you don't collect on it?" Roades shot back. He shouldered his duffel and headed to the door. "I'm on my way over. Gas up."

"Man, you know I have a checklist to go over before I fly. The body, the equipment..."

"We both know damn well that you've already done those checks earlier today." Cohen was the most conscientious pilot he knew, aware that a lot of small aircraft went down for stupid reasons that could be avoided.

"You know how to push a man. You should become a team leader."

"Maybe once my brother retires, I will. I'll be there in fifteen minutes."

The road from his family's home to Cohen's was the same one they took to go to their cabin in the bayou. He'd considered hiding out there for weeks but something had been stopping him. Now he knew what it was.

At the cabin, there was no cell service unless he had the satellite phone, and he'd relinquished it along with his position on the Knight Ops team while on

31

probation. Which meant Carissa never would have reached him.

Knights didn't believe in coincidence, and Roades sure as hell was a Knight.

Carissa's beautiful image hung in his mind, her heart-shaped face and piercing dark eyes beckoning him from hundreds of miles away.

I'm coming, Carissa. Whatever you need from me, I'm at your service.

Once more, that slow burn took up residence in his groin. Too bad the things he wanted to give probably weren't the ones she would ask for.

Six hours later the plane touched down on an abandoned runway of the military base that had cleared out after the hurricane. In the pilot's seat, Cohen looked at him. "How you getting where you need to go?"

"Don't worry. I got it from here." He unsealed the door and climbed out of the cockpit. He paused to look back in at his buddy, holding out his fist. Cohen bumped knuckles with him and gave him a crooked grin.

"You always were a daredevil. I swear you should have been a spy dropping into enemy territory."

He practically was. Carissa and her family weren't exactly on friendly terms after what he'd done to her.

"Thanks again, Cohen."

"Call if you need me to come back for you. I'm retired now."

Roades lifted a brow skeptically. "Sure you are."

Cohen shot him a private smile and then nodded. "See you soon, Knight. Godspeed."

Roades closed the hatch door, shouldered his duffel again and started walking. The dawn was just rising in the east, giving him enough light to see the weeds sprouting through the cracks of the cement on the abandoned airstrip.

Chapter Three

Carissa slipped back into the clinic and dropped the bag she was carrying. The contents were worth more than her life, and that was exactly what she was putting on the line every time she went to visit Angel.

"What choice do I have?" she murmured and unzipped the bag.

The inside was stuffed with all the medicines of all types. Things her patients needed.

Maybe she should take her own advice to Juanita and get the hell out of Puerto Rico and to the mainland. There at least she could get a job, start over.

That meant leaving her cousin and little brother behind, but Hernan was avoiding her and Mari could do for herself.

The other times she'd traded for the medicines, the crates she held in her possession had been enough of a payment. Now Angel was making other demands.

The door opening had her zipping the bag quickly and turning to see another neighbor, an older woman who'd been in the throes of cancer treatment when the clinic closed. The next town over had a facility, but Mrs. Galarza was not about to leave the world she knew and loved, even if it was destroyed from the natural disaster.

Carissa felt that familiar sinking feeling, like she was on the Titanic and knowing the only option was to hold tight and wait it out.

Or hope for rescue.

"Hello, Mrs. Galarza." Her voice was overly bright. "Come in and sit down."

The woman crossed the space and sank to the chair. She set her bag in her lap and then reached in to pull out a loaf of freshly baked bread wrapped in paper. Their regular appointment usually ended in Carissa having a full bread box, and for that she was grateful.

"I only got the one loaf this week. I'm sorry, dear." Mrs. Galarza's expression hung.

Carissa's heart went out to her, and she settled a hand on the woman's shoulder. "One is more than enough."

"I don't know how it could be. And I'd like to know how you're getting the medicine I need."

Carissa waved her off. "I manage. Now, let's set this loaf right here where it won't dry out in the sun." As she lay the bread to the side, the scents of yeast made her realize she'd forgotten breakfast in her hurry to meet Angel again and get the things she'd forgotten the previous day.

While Carissa gathered the medicines for Mrs. Galarza and placed them into a bag, she couldn't help but wonder how it would feel to not run these errands anymore. To not trade illegally and pray she wasn't caught.

She gripped the bag of medicine for a second, staring at nothing. Then Mrs. Galarza spoke, and Carissa turned with a smile.

"I've had a bit more energy of late." The older woman sprang from the chair and reached for the bag. "I appreciate these pills, Carissa girl. I really do."

"I wish I could get more than a week's worth at a time." The sample packs ran out fast.

She waved in dismissal. "Next time I'll bring you two loaves of bread and maybe some *quesitos*."

Carissa smiled at the mention of the pastries but she didn't feel it. Once the woman left, she massaged her aching temples and tried to focus her mind for the day. First, she needed to lock up the medicines she'd just received. Then—

The door opened again. Carissa dropped her hand abruptly and turned with a smile.

The smile fell before it appeared, and her heart did a wild tango.

Roades.

Her breath hitched, and her entire body trembled with the need to go to the man she'd fallen in love with so long ago and never stopped thinking about since.

His broad shoulders took up the entire doorway. When he stepped over the threshold, he ducked. With a shock, she realized he'd grown several inches since his teen years. He wore all black, his snug T-shirt showcasing muscles he'd never had before. And those cargo pants hung perfectly low on his hips.

But it was his eyes that really slayed her. They were deep and penetrating. They made her remember things, long ago buried.

The morning light streamed through the windows to beam over his ruggedly handsome features. His nose had a slight bump on the bridge, making her think he'd broken it at some point.

Her gaze moved over those lips that looked so hard but were incredibly tender, to his jaw, more angled than before and dark with beard growth.

Her stomach flipped again, filling with a liquid heat that was all too familiar when it came to having Roades in front of her.

She had to get a grip on her rioting emotions. He was here—somehow her ten-second phone call had summoned him to her door and now she had to pretend that he hadn't been her whole world at one time.

Dragging in a deep breath, she asked, "What happened to you?"

He raised a hand, fingers long and inciting visions of them on her body, and probed the edge of his bruised and swollen eye. "Had a tough walk in."

His voice had matured too, grown grittier.

She spun to her first-aid cabinet, gesturing to the chair. "Sit down and I'll see what I can do for the swelling."

He didn't move immediately, and she felt his hot gaze burning into her back. Or maybe her backside. Oh God, why had she called Roades? She had only been thinking of putting an end to Hernan's bad business and not about what Roades being here would mean to her.

Because, if she was honest, it meant everything. Her stupid little fool heart was pattering far too fast for a man who'd left her steps away from the altar.

Then she'd never heard from again.

She collected antiseptic and gauze to treat the cut on his cheekbone and an ice pack. She opened the package and shook it to activate the cold. He was so near, watching her, those dark eyes never moving from her face as she tried to conceal the fact that her hands were shaking.

For the first time, she wished she'd taken a few extra minutes on her appearance. She wore old jeans and a white blouse knotted at the waist, and her hair was in a messy bun piled high on her head. She felt escaped tendrils brushing her jaw.

Avoiding his gaze, she fixed her stare on his black eye. "Only a big, meaty fist could do this sort of damage," she said.

He grunted. The sound filtered through her like the warmth of a hundred summer days after being cast into the Antarctic.

She steadied her trembling hand and dabbed antiseptic on the gauze. When she gently pressed it to Roades' skin, he didn't even flinch.

But her insides were jiggling like pudding at touching this man again. At seventeen, she'd thought him adult. His serious demeanor had always made him seem older than his years. Now she realized a few years had really made huge differences in him.

Like how big he was.

And manly.

She winced as she cleaned the cut. "Sorry if I'm hurting you."

He didn't respond, and she darted a glance at his face to find his stare on her, steady. Searching.

Her breath trickled out of her.

"You're lucky this didn't break your orbital bone."

"I wasn't too concerned for my safety. He got a lucky punch."

Looking at him, no wonder he wasn't afraid.

"What is this place? Some sort of clinic?"

She nodded, swiping away a bit more blood, allowing the antiseptic to clear away the dried stuff. "The clinic in town closed after the hurricane and I have a lot of people coming to me for help."

"Are you trained?"

She looked into his eyes. "I'm a nurse."

His Adam's apple slid up and down his thick, tanned throat. "Your skills must have come in handy. This place isn't the same at all."

"Yes, there's a lot of damage. You should have seen it in the days after the hurricane. A lot of cleanup has taken place, though we have far to go."

Their conversation seemed surreal. They were discussing anything but why she'd called him and how either of them had lived their lives in the years since seeing each other.

This bigger, brighter version of Roades didn't seem in any hurry to speak about it, though, so she bit her tongue and cleaned away the last of the blood. Then she pressed some gauze over the wound followed by the ice pack.

"Hold this in place."

He took over holding the ice pack. When she started to lower her hand, he caught it in his free one. His grip warm, rough. Her eyes threatened to close at the mere sensation.

He captured her gaze and held it prisoner. Her breaths came faster.

"Now that I'm no longer bleeding, it's time to talk, Carissa."

* * * * *

40

Slowly, she extricated her hand from his grasp and stepped back. Roades couldn't stop looking at her. The changes in her were striking. The same Carissa but enhanced — plumper lips, more curves. She was more feminine.

She had the same lean legs that had driven him out of his mind at seventeen. Now her sex appeal drove him to new heights.

She brushed a loose tendril of hair from her high cheekbone and riveted her glimmering black eyes on him. He'd always thought her eyes held her entire soul, and now it almost hurt him to meet them. He saw she'd experienced pain since he'd walked out of her life, and it was impossible not to take that on his shoulders.

"Can I get you a drink or anything to eat?" she asked. Her hand landed on the counter and her knuckles whitened with tension.

He shook his head. "Tell me why you called me."

She stiffened a bit at his command, and he realized she wasn't used to this version of him. He'd had a lot of living in their time apart too, and the man he was now was one tough motherfucker. The assholes who'd jumped him during his walk here had learned that the hard way.

When she dropped her gaze to her feet, his heart recalled every sweet thing she'd ever said to him. How she loved him, never wanted to be parted from him. And dammit, he'd felt the same.

If his father hadn't pried them apart, he would have married her.

Then he wouldn't be a Marine or involved with OFFSUS. It was impossible to gauge how he felt about any of that, so he pushed it from his mind.

"Start from the beginning. Where are your parents?"

Her head snapped up. "They're gone. Killed in a car accident four months after you left."

All the air exited his lungs in a rush. He'd broken her and then left her to deal alone with her parents' loss.

"What about Hernan?"

She drew her shoulders back. "I raised him."

"Alone?" Part of him didn't believe a woman like Carissa was single. He'd thought about it a lot during the flight and long walk here, but in the end, he'd decided it didn't matter if she was married. She'd called him for a reason, and he was going to help.

"With the help of my cousin Mari."

Relief washed over him, but he wasn't going to recognize that. He nodded. "I remember Mari."

"She lives here with me, but Hernan…"

He looked at her harder. The change in her voice, the slight wobble alerted him to the reason he was here pointing to Hernan.

"Well, Hernan was *bueno* for many years. But since the hurricane and the people fleeing, the businesses closed..." She trailed off, pinching the bridge of her nose. A nose Roades had kissed so many times he'd lost count.

He lowered the ice pack. "Now he's back to his old ways?"

She bit down on her lower lip. The action made Roades' cock jerk, and it was all he could do to remain seated and not stand and yank her into his arms.

After an agonizing second of his internal battle, she nodded. "He's stopping the free water supply from reaching the people."

"Stopping it how?"

She shrugged. "I don't know. Only that he's charging for it."

"Fuck."

She stared at him, eyes wide. "I shouldn't have called you, Roades. I'm sorry you made the trip down here when you must have other obligations. I just didn't know what to do. Hernan isn't going to listen to me. I can't even find him."

"First, you didn't take me away from anything—I had some free time. And secondly, you did right in calling me." Hernan was a little punk back in the day, and Roades had spent some time with him in hopes of showing him that life wasn't all gangs and wrongdoings. That it wasn't cool to commit crimes like Hernan's friends believed.

And lording over the water supply to a town as ravaged as this one was wrong to the *nth* degree.

Carissa wouldn't meet his gaze.

"What else aren't you telling me?" His gut instincts were never off, and he knew Carissa better than he cared to admit.

Her eyes flicked to a cupboard and then back to him. "I need medicines. For my patients. I went this morning but what I need…"

"Yes?" he prompted.

"I get them off the black market."

Jesus. "The black market?"

She nodded. "See, I have something to… trade."

His hand snapped into a fist. If she was talking about her body, he was going to explode.

In a rush, she said, "A doctor friend of mine fled to the mainland after the disaster, but he left me with crates of narcotics. Oxycodone and fentanyl. Things people abuse. And you're going to think terribly of me, but I've been trading the crates for medicines and supplies for my people."

Oh God. His dear, sweet Carissa was embroiled in a dangerous game with dangerous people.

"And now these people you trade with are saying the crates aren't enough?"

She nodded.

His thigh muscles burned with the effort to remain calmly seated and not jump up to grab Carissa and pull her against his chest. To shelter and protect.

"*Mon coeur*," he said slowly, his Cajun drawl sticking out like a rhinoceros in a city compared to her accent. "What is it they're asking of you?"

She looked away and pushed out a breath. "Sex," she stated simply.

Roades leaped to his feet, the ice pack hitting the floor. The gauze she'd placed over the cut temporarily fluttered to land on his boot, but he ignored it and closed the distance between them.

"Like hell. Like hell!" His roar made her step back and her spine came up against the wall. Fury quaked within him, and he fisted his hands. "Tell me where."

She shook her head, and Roades gripped her elbows, towering over her.

"*Mon coeur*, if you don't tell me, I'll go looking for them myself and you won't want to hear what happens then."

She felt fragile in his hold. The urge to protect strengthened by ten times.

"Don't protect these assholes," he said.

"That isn't it. They move around."

"How do you find them then?"

"I sort of guess between the places where they hole up."

45

"Give me the locations." Her lips were so close, so plump and inviting. One dip of his head and he'd have them under his. Fuck, he wanted it bad.

She searched his face as if trying to tell if he was a stranger or the man she knew. He was both, and there was no way to tell her that. Explaining the things he'd seen and done, the battles he'd engaged in and put an end to, and the things he'd fucked up in his life—including leaving her—were beyond him.

"Roades." Her voice came out on a plea. "You have no choice but to take me with you. But know this, if I didn't truly need these medicines desperately, I wouldn't take you there. The people I'm dealing with…"

Would be dead in an hour, if he had anything to say about it. What they were doing was bad enough but asking Carissa for sex in trade?

His bowels turned to water at the thought that this could have happened before. That she might have given in to help her patients receive aid.

Curling his hand around her nape, Roades looked into her eyes. "Is this the first time they've made this demand of you?"

"Yes," she said at once.

Okay, so he might not have to kill them right away. He could wait for them to make a move first.

"I will take you there, Roades. But only because I need these pills for a little girl." She raised a hand, letting it linger over his chest, but did not touch him.

Battling the need to kiss her—claim her—he dropped his hand from her nape and stepped back. Still feeling the warmth of her body on his skin and the silky strands of her hand on his fingertips.

Putting a hand to his spine where his weapon was nestled, he turned for the door. "Let's go."

He wanted to get this over with and then deal with Hernan. But once those jobs were finished, more problems would crop up for Carissa. In her eyes, he saw the way life had beaten her down, and damn if he could leave her like that.

* * * * *

"Tell me you don't come here in the dark." Roades' rough tone washed over Carissa like a tidal wave on parched land, leaving her shaken, but his statement came through.

She tossed him a look over her shoulder and glimpsed the hard set of his jaw and narrowed eyes. He wasn't looking at her but beyond her, as if checking for danger. Not for the first time, she wondered what he did for a living that had not only packed so much muscle on him but given him such a hard demeanor.

He groaned. "You do come here in the dark."

No response was necessary as she moved down the alleyway. Between the tall buildings, sunlight didn't penetrate easily and if she didn't know better, she'd think it was dusk.

Looking around, she realized what Roades must be seeing—cracked pavement, junk piled in the path for people to hide behind. And no way out except a long run ahead.

He caught her by the shoulder, hand warm and heavy. He drew her to a stop and slipped around her. "I'm going first. My radars are going off."

She was faced with his back and even without a lot of sunlight, she made out the glide of muscle as he moved.

"Keep close."

"It's not all that dangerous, Roades. What do you do for a living anyway? Are you some kind of superhero expecting someone to jump out at you around every corner?"

He tossed her a look that bordered on wry.

Curiosity burned on her tongue but she didn't say more, because he raised a hand to silence her. He canted his head slightly as if listening hard. Then a door in one building opened and the head of the alley darkened as men poured out.

"Goddammit," Roades drawled, sounding too nonchalant like they weren't suddenly facing down the danger she'd told him wasn't here.

Her heart slammed her ribs in a disjointed rhythm, and she plastered herself to his back. Then she realized the men could be Angel and his friends.

She peeked around Roades. "Angel?"

A harsh laugh sounded. "That you, *puta*? No, we drove that *Estupido* out. We took all his goods too." The laughs multiplied as the man's friends chimed in.

A couple men stepped toward Roades and Carissa, and the unmistakable gleam of knives being pulled had Carissa twisting the fabric of Roades' shirt. He reached behind him and squeezed her hand.

Then he shoved her into some junk. "Get down. Stay small!"

She barely had time to get her bearings before his boots thudded pavement. Wait—he was running straight into a group of guys wielding knives?

A cry broke from her, and she covered her head with her hands, listening for screams and sounds of violence. The first grunt of pain hit her, and she darted her head out from behind a twisted piece of metal that might have once been a car door.

What she saw made her jaw drop.

Roades moving like a panther, and dressed all in black like one too, as he did a dance of what could only be a martial art. She knew nothing of the varieties but he was clearly trained.

A click of a weapon sounded. "Don't come any closer, man!" someone yelled in Spanish.

Ignoring the warning, Roades continued forward. Men came at him, one latching himself onto Roades' back while another jabbed at him with a lethal blade.

Carissa issued a strangled cry, but before it was completely past her lips, Roades had the situation handled. The man with the knife lying in a heap, probably sporting a broken arm and the one on his back flipped over his head and his spine smashed into the pavement.

Tremors broke over her. What the hell was going on? Was she really seeing this?

Awed, a bit frightened and a lot turned on, she watched from her hiding spot as he singlehandedly kicked no less than five thugs' asses. One was still moving on the ground, and Roades quickly dispatched him so he no longer even twitched.

He stood there a moment, arms loose at his sides but hands still fisted. She couldn't even blink because looking away from him would mean she'd miss something, and she definitely did not want to do that.

When he slowly pivoted, he said, "Stay there another minute while I check something."

He walked to the door and opened it. Seconds later, he closed it and came back to her, reaching a hand down into the pile of junk to pull her out.

She looked at his hand, and there wasn't a speck of blood on it, but she knew without a doubt this was a hand that could kill — or *had* killed.

An uneven breath puffed past her lips as she allowed him to draw her to a stand. She couldn't meet his eyes and stared at his chest. So much power was harnessed behind that black cotton shirt. Power she hadn't guessed at and didn't know how to process.

This man was not the Roades she'd known.

Christ, she wouldn't even look at him. And he still wanted to put someone through the side of the building for trying to attack them. If Carissa had come here alone…

He growled and tightened his hold on her hand. She followed him to the door he'd opened. Inside was nothing more than a back room of some abandoned business with boxes and tables piled with loot. One glance had told him this was what Carissa had been looking for.

When she saw the haul in front of her, she gasped.

"Take what you need."

He wanted to throw her over his shoulder and get her on Cohen's plane back to Louisiana. Fuck this disaster area and fuck Hernan. Let the man come to his own end. Roades wanted to bust out that little punk's teeth for leaving his sister to fend for herself. Any brother worth a fucking damn would have gotten her to safety, not gone his own way while she repeatedly took chances.

Carissa moved a hand toward some items. Roades reached past her and snatched up a box, swiping everything on the table into it. "Fuck it. We're taking it all."

She made a squeaking noise but said nothing. She had to be reeling from what she'd seen him just do, and for that he was sorry. But he'd do it again for her.

At the door, she clutched at his arm. "We can't take it all—they'll come after us."

He thought of the bodies littering the ground. "I'm not worried about that."

"Is this what you'll do to Hernan?" Tears were in her voice, and he turned, softening at once.

"He's your brother. I'll try to talk sense. And if he won't listen?" He looked through the open door at the nearest man lying in an unnatural position, though he wasn't dead. None of them were. "Then I'll kick Hernan's ass too. He deserves it from what you say and isn't that why you brought me down here? C'mon."

He didn't wait for her to walk around the limbs scattering the pavement but reeled her close with an arm around her waist and lifted her. With Carissa's soft body snug against him and the box balanced in the other hand, he navigated to the head of the alley and made his way into the sunlight again.

He set her down and she tipped her head back to meet his stare—at last. Electric need zapped his system, and he didn't give a damn about what had come before or brought them to this point in time.

He swooped in and kissed her.

A small gasp escaped her, and he deepened the kiss, angling his head to fully taste every square inch of her plump lips. That mouth of hers had been driving him crazy for years, haunting his dreams so he'd wake with a hard-on no man could fall back asleep with. Then Roades had let his fantasies take over.

But he was finished with fantasies—he had the real deal in front of him.

He yanked her onto tiptoe, one hand on her firm round ass. She parted her lips and he plunged his tongue inside her mouth.

Sweet fucking heaven.

Dear God, how had he lived without this for so many years? How had he forgotten? Her flavor, pure woman, was something that rushed back at him and after drowning for so long, he was finally breaking the surface and gulping real air.

He slid his tongue across hers again and again until she began to respond with throaty moans and small flicks of her own tongue.

He let out another growl, and she responded with a quiet mewl.

"Hell, I'm a goner for sure now. That sound you just made…" He ran his hand up her spine to her nape, guiding her closer. What he wouldn't give to drop the box and yank her fully into his arms, but he was afraid of who'd run up and try to steal it. He didn't want to have to break someone's neck in Carissa's presence.

Though adrenaline coursed through him at the mere thought of what she might have walked into if he hadn't been here, he had no doubts about what would have happened to her.

Drawing her tighter, he pulled from the kiss. "I want you home to safety and a promise that you'll never attempt to go out looking to trade without me again. Then I want your clothes off."

She stared up at him, lips swollen from his assault, and damn if he could feel sorry about it. Her eyes were blurred with desire. Then they cleared and she stepped back. "We have some things to discuss."

"Yeah, we do. Like why the hell you would think it's okay to deal with criminals like this without a bodyguard."

She stiffened. "I do what I must. You would too in my situation."

He studied her. Dark hair tumbling down from its perch on top of her head and enough grit in the set of her spine to help her survive... well, this.

She started walking in the direction of her house. What he remembered of the small town was nothing like what he saw before him, and it broke his heart. Those weeks he'd spent here with her had been the best of his life. Street parties, music and so much loving. Carissa wrapped in his arms as he fell asleep each night and a promise to love her forever on his lips.

He dragged in a deep breath through his nose and adjusted his grip on the box so he could take her by the hand and still make a grab for his weapon if it came to that.

"What was that back there?" she asked after a few minutes.

"That was a gang of thugs who apparently overtook the thug you regularly deal with, if I'm guessing correctly."

She side-eyed him. "I mean the thing you did. Was that karate?"

"I call it Roadese. My own brand of martial arts."

"You've trained in many?"

He didn't know how much to tell her, and especially out here in the open streets where somebody could easily overhear. "Let's say I'm proficient enough to mash the arts together into a bastard skill set."

She didn't speak for more long minutes, and he grew mesmerized by the sway of her hips and the length of hair on her back, fallen from the confinements of the bun when he'd thrown her into the junk to keep her safe.

"Did you kill them?"

Her question caught him off-guard, and he chuckled. "No."

"Are you sure? That one looked like he might have a broken neck."

"Just the angle he fell. Believe me, I'd know a dead man if I saw it."

Now he'd gone and terrified her. The lights in her eyes dimmed and she shied away, putting distance between them.

He touched her shoulder to bring her back to him both emotionally and physically. He shouldn't want to keep her so close, since he'd be leaving again after this was done or he was called back to the Knight Ops—whichever came first. But he wanted her, dammit. His cock was still throbbing with need and he'd imagined her naked at least half a dozen times since telling her he wanted her clothes off.

"Look, I promise I'll tell you anything you want to know once we reach your house." He turned his head to look at a family camped out in a makeshift shelter on a sidewalk, small kids sitting cross-legged, tossing a pebble back and forth across the cracks of the concrete. Their faces were dirty and they looked hungry.

"Dammit." He reached for his wallet and stepped up to the mother, who sat nearby looking as downtrodden as any human could. He handed her a wad of bills, and the woman burst into tears.

She jumped to her feet, noisily thanking him in Spanish that he followed with an increasing amount of discomfort. He didn't want to be recognized for helping the family—and now they were drawing a crowd.

He disentangled himself from her hold around his neck and gave her a nod and wave.

He took a few steps before he realized Carissa still stood rooted back on the sidewalk. He twitched his head for her to catch up and she did, a dazed look on her face.

"Roades, that was…"

"The least I could do."

"I was going to say kind. And a lot of money."

He shrugged, his shirt feeling suddenly too tight across his shoulders. He felt like he was back in Afghanistan watching the war unravel the people and their lives until there was nothing left but bombed buildings and hopelessness.

Except a natural disaster had done the bombing and either the efforts hadn't yet reached the island or nobody gave a shit about the people who were left.

He jammed his fingers through his hair and squinted as the sun worked its way higher into the sky. God, he was tired. He'd walked all night and kicked no less than nine men's asses. He'd also experienced an emotion he hadn't in a long time.

Fear.

When it came to himself or his team, fear almost never arose. He was always certain they'd take care of business. But knowing Carissa was here doing this alone… God.

He swung his head right and left, keeping on alert as they walked the rest of the distance back to her house. When she stepped up on the stoop and threw him a mischievous smile, he caught his breath.

That look he recognized all too well.

"If you don't get that door open in the next second, I'm going to beat it down," he said.

She made a noise that was somewhere between giggle and snort. She used the key and twisted the handle. Inside smelled like all the things he remembered about Carissa years ago. The scent of drying herbs and something spicy that was almost medicinal.

She stood before him, all curves and dark eyes and shining hair. His heart skipped a beat as he set down the box and took her into his arms.

"Was that under a second?" she said, looking up into his eyes.

He nodded, raking his gaze over her beautiful face again and again, not quite certain he wasn't fast asleep in his bed at home and none of this had happened, that he wasn't really here with the old love of his life again.

She raised a hand to curl it around the back of his neck, an action that shouldn't arouse him, but damn if he had any control over his cock.

"First, that promise." His demand was quiet.

She stared at his chest for a long minute and then finally nodded.

He groaned. "Next step is to get your clothes off," he murmured before claiming her mouth once again.

Chapter Four

Carissa's body was tuning up to Roades' nearness — *tuning in.* She hadn't been with anyone in a long time, but this was far more than being horny. Her body knew this man even if her mind didn't totally understand who he had become.

He slanted his mouth across hers, slick tongue probing the depths and making her insides quiver with a need to feel him between her legs once again. She clung to his shoulders, learning the carved muscles rivaling an action hero's. Somehow the images of him as a younger Roades meshed with her new ones and now she could barely recall a time he wasn't this huge beast of a man.

A faint cry broke from her when he eased his hand around the curve of her ass.

"Fuck, I missed this ass." His gritty tone was swallowed by another kiss when she went on tiptoe to take his mouth.

The house was empty, Mari at her job working an early shift. And that was good, because Carissa would never be able to remain silent once Roades got her into bed.

Passion swelled, curled and broke over her like a wave hitting the shores.

"C'mere, *mon coeur*." She'd missed him calling her the endearment that meant *my heart*.

He hooked both hands under her buttocks and lifted her as if she weighed nothing. She looped her thighs around him and held onto his broad shoulders as he carried her through the house.

When he reached the door to what was her former room, he paused.

She shook her head. "I have my parents' old room."

"They're gonna roll in their graves."

She didn't know whether to laugh or regret they weren't here. As he carried her through the door, a sudden shock of what she was doing hit.

She was with Roades again.

After all these years of pain and missing him like she'd miss her own limb if it were cut off, she was in his arms.

And he was kissing the hell out of her.

The kiss turned carnal in a second, and he dropped her to the bed and followed her down before she could even adjust her position on the mattress. He locked his hand on the back of her head and dragged her thigh across his hips, splaying her on his leg.

The urge to rock against the steely muscle was too much, and she succumbed. Pushing down on his hard thigh, she gasped as her pussy flooded with need.

"God, you're gorgeous. More gorgeous than you were years ago. I've missed so much." He planted a big hand on her ass and dragged her down on his leg again. She moaned. He growled.

"I need to see you without clothes, Roades." Her plea came out breathy, almost inaudible. But he heard.

Drawing her to the side, he gave her free rein of his body. She reached for the hem of his T-shirt, tugging it free from his waistband and up over sculpted six-pack abs that made her blush just from looking at them.

Before she could remove his shirt, he flipped her onto her back, hovering over her. Seconds passed as their gazes said all the words neither could seem to conjure.

"Take off my clothes, please," she whispered.

If he walked away from her again, at this very moment, she'd be devastated. And that was a very dangerous thing. She couldn't afford to be in more emotional turmoil than she already was. But one night with the man she'd loved enough to want to marry once upon a time… that was worth any twinges of the heart she might experience afterward.

There wouldn't be regrets, though. Not more than she already had after being left with only his picture in her mind.

His biceps bulged as he bore his weight over her. His thick hair fell across his forehead. "Carissa…"

He looked about to say something she didn't want to hear, be it about their past or present. Either way, she didn't want to listen.

She pressed a fingertip to his lips and then reached under his shirt, exploring those abs she'd only gotten a glimpse of. Then up over bump after bump of muscle to reach his hard pecs.

A shiver rolled through her.

He bowed his head over her, and she was reminded of times he'd gone to mass with her and bowed it in prayer.

After a long second, he raised his head and met her gaze. "I want to go slow with you. To kiss and stroke every inch of your body until you're screaming for me. But..." His throat worked. "I can't. I can't go slow."

A trickle of air left her lungs, pushed out by relief. She'd feared he'd call a halt to all of their foreplay and leave her aching.

To help him along, she grabbed the bottom of her shirt and yanked it up and off. Her hair fell across the pillow, and his stare traveled over it before landing on her face. Roving over her features to her throat and lower to her breasts.

She wished she had a prettier bra for him to eye up, but he didn't seem to mind if the bulge against her thigh was anything to go by.

His eyelids closed and then he opened them again. "Hell, *mon coeur*."

Throwing away all caution, she took his hand and placed it over her breast.

A shudder ran through him, and his eyes hooded in that way she remembered and sometimes woke with in her mind, as if she'd dreamed about this very look all night long.

His hand lay on her breast, warm and heavy. Then he caressed her mound. Her nipple hardened instantly, and he found it with a forefinger, rubbing back and forth until it was straining and small gasps escaped her.

"Still so responsive."

He watched her face intently as he strummed her nipple over and over. When he eased his hand along the band of her bra to the clasp on her spine, she held her breath. How long had she needed his touch? More so in the years after than before. She'd been so young—would this encounter be different?

It had to be. And that was okay.

She arched to give him access to the clasp. He sprung it and slowly stripped the fabric from her. When the warm air kissed her skin, both nipples pebbled. Or maybe that was from Roades' gaze being on her.

"Fuck. Fucking hell." He dropped his head between her breasts, and she held him there with her fingers tangled in his hair. He drew five deep breaths while she wondered what it was this man had seen in his short life. He was much changed and his skills on the streets verified he was trained in the military or the like.

She ran her hands down the planes of his back, mentally picturing how it would look. What she wouldn't give to just stand back and look at him, drink it all in. Call her perverted but seeing a beautiful man who worked hard on his body was transcendent. And if she could get him in the sunlight, even better…

He strummed one nipple.

"Pinch them, Roades. Please."

He groaned and then his questing fingertips closed around one nipple. "I forgot you liked this. Jesus." He ran the rough, beard-stubbled angle of his jaw across her sensitive skin, making her gasp.

When he sucked her other nipple into his mouth, she stopped breathing altogether.

With soft pulls of his lips, he tormented her while tweaking her other nipple with his fingers. Then he switched and she lost herself in the pull of pleasure between her thighs. Much more of this and she might after barely making it to second base.

Just when she didn't think she could endure more, he slid downward, kissing her abdomen. She dug her fingers into his hair and guided him as he traced zigzags across her flesh.

"Beautiful. Soft." His murmur sent shivers through her.

For a man who couldn't go slow, he sure as hell was doing a fine job. She grabbed the cloth between his shoulder blades and pulled his shirt off. He gave her a dark look full of intensity she'd never seen before. What kind of lover was Roades now? She hoped to find out.

But part of her waited for the boot to drop and for him to draw back, to retreat into himself and not finish what he'd started.

Urgency made her hands shake as she tossed his shirt aside and touched him.

"God, Carissa." He acted as if… as if he hadn't been touched for as long as she hadn't.

Looking the way he did, that was not possible. But none of that mattered because she was going to show him just how much she wanted him in this minute.

She leaned up and captured his mouth. Kissing, teasing with nibbles and bites on his lower lip. Then twisting her tongue around his for many heartbeats. When he popped the button at her waist and slid her zipper down, she kissed him with all the pent-up desire inside her.

Suddenly, he yanked free, staring down at her, panting.

"*Mon coeur.*"

Don't say it's a mistake. It might be but who cares.

"What is it?" she whispered, searching his rugged features for answers before he spoke. She'd guarded her heart very well after he left her, and she still had a wall up. But that didn't mean one word from him couldn't tear her apart all over again.

"I don't trust myself not to hurt you."

Her breath hitched. "Are you into some dark stuff like BDSM or something?"

A harsh laugh left him. "Nothing like that. But right now tying you up sounds like the best thought I've had in years."

She giggled and held her hands out, wrists together. "I'm ready."

"*Mon coeur*, you don't know what you're getting into with me." He dropped his mouth to her breast again and she gave herself up to sensation. Each stroke of his tongue, wet and slippery, sent her into paroxysms of need. He managed to get her pants off and took her panties with them.

Pulsating now, she waited for him to put his hands, lips, cock where she needed them most. But he didn't touch her.

Just leaned back on his knees to look at her.

"You're different," he said softly, a pang of pain in his voice.

"So are you." She cut her gaze over his bare chest and shoulders, down to the dark trail of hair leading into his cargo pants. She wet her lips, and he groaned.

In a flash, he leaped off the bed and stood alongside, watching her face as he shucked boots, socks, pants and lastly, boxers.

Her need spiked at seeing him in all his full glory, with the sun from the windows streaming over his muscles, creating light and shadows in all the right places.

His eyes hooded again as he tore open a condom produced from some pocket and he stroked it into place. The veins snaking up and down his forearm made her wish she could watch him do that more often.

Finished with inhibitions, she let her thighs fall open in invitation.

He didn't hesitate. Pressing her down into the mattress, the light fur on his chest skimming her hardened nipples as he poised his cock at the V of her thighs.

Their gazes locked and he pushed in with one hard glide, completely filling her.

Her body stretched, burning almost, but in the best way possible. He fell still at the invasion into her body but stared at her lips as if they'd done him wrong.

"Roades." Her voice brought his gaze up to hers again.

He started to move. In seconds, she saw why he'd held himself in check—he was an animal in bed with her. Rocking into her hard, shoving her up the bed. Each plunge of his cock had her crying out, the pinnacle of release just in reach, she was sure of it.

His kisses were bruising. Then tender. Alternating until she didn't know what to expect next.

When he locked the length of her hair around his fist and yanked her head back to suck on her neck and breasts, she lost all sense of reality. The years separating them vanished and it was only Roades.

He fucked her faster, churning his hips. The bed strained in protest but she could barely make out anything over the rough growls rumbling through her lover's chest.

Suddenly, he released his grip on her hair and thrust his fingers between their bodies. The rough pads of his fingertips found her clit immediately. He pressed down, and she cried out. Juices flooded, and her body clamped down.

He groaned in response, and she grasped him to her harder, wanting everything from him, including a release like she'd never had before.

Because she was on the verge of that very thing.

He flicked her clit with each thrust of his cock, and it was too much. Too good. Too—

She tensed as her orgasm hit. A tempest swept up her body. And its name was Roades.

* * * * *

The tight clench of Carissa's body around him made his balls draw up. The tingle at the base of his spine struck, and he pounded his release into her. Each spurt timed to his cock sinking into her body.

Bliss spread through him and he couldn't think, just move. As the last of his release left him, he slowed. Small rasps still came from Carissa with each strum of his fingers on her clit. The sweet little pearl needed a good sucking, and soon.

First, he needed to catch his breath. And if he was honest, sleep. The toll on his body was more than he cared to admit, but this little vixen had just sapped him of more than his cum.

He rolled to the side and took her with him, still inside her hot body. When he pulled his fingers out from between them and licked her juices off one, she shivered.

He looked into her eyes. Fuck.

"Did I hurt you?"

She blinked. "Did I sound hurt?"

He barked out a laugh, the sound foreign after the weeks of probation and stress he'd endured. His heart softened at seeing the stunning woman locked in his arms, his cock still stretching her tight pussy.

He brushed her thick hair off her cheekbone. "You're more beautiful now than you were then. I don't know how that's possible."

"You've grown up a lot. I don't know how *that's* possible."

"Are you talking about my behavior? Because I happen to think I was pretty damn mature at seventeen."

She smiled at the teasing in his voice. "You were."

"But my brothers always tell me they didn't think I'd stop being such a pipsqueak."

"How is your family?"

He was still hard but slipped free of Carissa's body. She curled onto one side to look at him.

Dear God, he'd missed this. Talking to her. Learning what was in her mind.

He couldn't let himself get so close, though he feared that had already happened. How stupid of him to claim her body in such a way. He knew how damned tenderhearted she was, and he'd left lasting bruises on her when he'd gone. He couldn't risk doing that again—but probably already had.

"My family's just as crazy and demanding as ever." More so, with four of them in Knight Ops, one sister a Marine and the other with a tendency to choose the wrong men.

But Carissa knew nothing of his situation or work, and maybe that was for the best.

Her body glistened with the afterglow of their lovemaking, and—

Shit. Lovemaking? He definitely needed to put the brakes on sooner rather than later. Coming to her aid—and then coming inside her—had worn him down in ways he couldn't allow.

70

He sat up and swung his legs off the bed, reaching for his boxers. He went dead still. The faint knocking wasn't coming from the front door but around back in Carissa's clinic.

"Damn!" She jumped from the bed and started throwing on her clothes. "That'll be a patient."

"Coming!" she yelled loud enough the person could probably hear through the thin walls of her home.

Roades threw out an arm to stop her as she rounded the bed, topless. "You're not going to the door alone."

"Well, of course not like this! Where's *mi camisa*?" She searched the floor and then leaned over to snatch up her shirt, giving him more lurid fantasies.

The knocking ensued, and she ran out of the bedroom while pulling her shirt into place.

"Goddammit." He grabbed his pants and had them on and buttoned, regardless of the condom he hadn't disposed off and his still-hard cock.

He stomped through the house to catch Carissa before she opened the door on what could be a shit storm after what he'd just done to those men back in the alley.

He grabbed her before she reached the door, spinning her to face him. "You could be walking into something bad, Carissa. Think of what just happened out there."

The color drained from her face.

71

"Let me go first."

"But if it's dear old Miss Juanita, she'll have a heart attack seeing a big..." She waved a hand over his physique, and damn if his body wasn't reacting again. He could lift her over his cock and pin her to the wall.

No.

He had to shake himself to clear his thoughts and adjusted his statement. "I'm going first."

There was no entrance to the clinic from the house, and he had to walk outside. On guard, he swept the perimeter but detected no threats. Carissa, and probably Mari too, had cleared the yard of the smaller stuff that had washed over when the hurricane hit but there were still heavy objects he could take care of. He circled those and around to the back of the house.

The clinic was a shed of sorts scabbed together out of whatever scrap lumber could be found, and he wasn't sure if it had been added on while her parents were still alive or if Carissa had managed it out of pure necessity following the disaster.

Some of the boards had peeling paint and some were raw, weathered gray. The door looked crooked, as did the older woman standing there.

She looked at him, startled.

He stared at her harder. "Luciana?"

She blinked and straightened. "*Dios mio,* it *is* you." She flattened a hand over her bony chest as

Roades stepped forward. He drew the older woman into a big hug, and she stepped back to gawp at his chest. "There's a lot of you now, dear."

Grinning, he moved to open the door for the woman he'd known from his stay here. The neighbor had been on Team Roades and had even championed him to Carissa's father when Roades had shown up begging for her hand. But now, time and events seemed to have ravaged her appearance.

She looked like the slightest ocean breeze would knock her over.

"Luciana." Carissa stepped around Roades, shooting him a look. "I've got what you need. Come inside."

She led the woman into the clinic and whether or not he was wanted there, he entered as well. He wasn't letting her out of his sight after what had happened in the alley. When those guys gained consciousness, they'd know where to find Carissa for sure. But killing them in front of her hadn't been an option for Roades, which was why he had to find them again and make sure they kept their distance— or else.

Yeah, she didn't need to know about the violence he was capable of. It was better if she continued to think of him as the young man she'd known years ago.

"Excuse me a minute," Carissa said to Luciana. She turned to Roades. "I need some time alone. Go get dressed," she whispered.

He eyed her and the flimsy door that even if she closed and locked it, would be no match for a set of thugs like the ones he'd just put in their places.

But he could see Carissa's glare wouldn't be wiped from her face until he followed her wishes. It took some effort, but he nodded and then turned for the house again. She'd managed to survive all these months without him and probably could handle herself better than he thought.

Before she closed the clinic door, he heard Juanita's voice ring out. "Roades is back? *Niña,* that's a lot of *pecho* for your hands!"

He chuckled. He'd leave them to discuss his chest.

Chapter Five

When Carissa finished with Juanita, doing her best to avoid the woman's gossiping questions about Roades and how he came to be here and —*gasp!*— shirtless, she saw the older woman outside.

Only to find Roades fully dressed and leaning against the side of the clinic. It seemed also he'd taken it upon himself to move some of the bigger items that littered her garden.

A warm tingle took up residence in her stomach, along with a wallop of anxiety.

He'd left her before and would again. Why had she let herself fall prey to his charms a second time around?

Stupid. So stupid.

She waited until Juanita was out of earshot before looking Roades in the eyes.

Another mistake—she shouldn't have done that. Those deep eyes of his always made her feel she was seeing something special just for her.

"Roades."

"Get your neighbor taken care of?" He pulled away from the wall and approached her with a slow roll of his muscles that was visual porn coming her direction.

She shook herself. "Roades, we need to stop and think about this. I—" She dropped her gaze to her hands. Drawing a deep breath, she let the words she'd been thinking since leaving the bed to fall from her tongue. "I shouldn't have slept with you."

He stopped his slow stalk and looked at her, face calm and something completely unreadable in his eyes. This was something she definitely couldn't deal with—she didn't know the real Roades, this Roades.

She'd jumped into bed with the man she remembered and damn, had he rekindled those fires with his knowledge of her body. She felt so predictable in her wants and needs, while she didn't feel she could offer him the same. He was a different person.

"Is that so?" His Cajun drawl got her every time. But she needed to steel herself against all the charms he threw her way like grenades. She felt the blasts deep in her body still, but there must be a way to defuse those feelings.

She nodded. "Yes, it was a mistake."

"How so?" He reached out and caught a tendril of her hair between his big fingers.

She couldn't think when he was touching her, even if she couldn't feel it. She stepped back.

He followed her.

"Didn't I make you come apart?"

Dieu, did he.

She couldn't start thinking about his hands on her, his mouth. The way he'd filled her so—

She came up against the clinic door and realized she'd been stepping backward with Roades pursuing her.

Pressing her hands against the wood for support, she straightened her spine. "I lost my head, Roades. After seeing you again and well…" She waved a hand at his physique, which only brought a smirk to his damned handsome face. She sucked in a breath and continued, "It was a mistake, a one-time affair."

The smirk vanished and he jerked his chin up. "Ah. So you're saying, *mon coeur*," he dragged out the word, pulling each syllable over her senses like a silken cord over her skin, "that you don't want more of the pleasures I can give you."

No. She wasn't saying that.

But she had to act like she didn't.

She nodded.

He braced his hands on the door on each side of her shoulders and leaned in. She gulped. When his warm breath washed over her cheek, it was all she could do to keep from turning her head, turning into his kiss.

"I guess I will have to keep my distance then, won't I?" His dark words vibrated in her soul even as his body language said something entirely different than his words.

Somehow, she managed a stiff nod.

He did a pushup off the door and turned for the house. Some people claimed the view from the top of Everest was the best in the world. Or from the depths of the Pacific Ocean on a coral reef.

But until those people had seen a muscled Knight man from behind in all its carved glory, they hadn't truly lived.

"Guess I'd better hurry up and find Hernan then," he called over his shoulder. "I'll get outta your hair."

He disappeared into the house, and she was left weak-kneed, clinging to the door for support. Back in the clinic while thwarting Juanita's new wedding plans for her and Roades, Carissa's thoughts on the matter had made perfect sense. Sleeping with Roades had been pure chemistry but now that it was out of their systems, she could see it for what it was and not make the same mistake.

Slowly, she drew away from the door and crossed the small patch of grass and into the house and caught her breath at the sound of trickling water.

Roades was cleaning up.

That big, naked man was standing naked in her bathroom, water splashing over his tanned flesh all the way down to soak the thatch of hair at the base of his cock.

She issued a feminine moan and immediately checked it.

What she needed was a set of earplugs. Then a blindfold.

There was only one answer to stop her insides from knotting — Hernan better show himself soon.

* * * * *

Carissa finished cleaning up the blood spilled around her clinic. The man who'd come in with an emergency had woken her earlier than usual and her adrenaline had left her wide awake.

The wound on his hand had required cleaning before she could even assess the damage. Once she'd seen the deep gash, she'd grabbed her needle and sutures and a syringe of local anesthetic.

While stitching the wound, she'd talked to the man calmly, asking questions about his family and job, where he'd sustained the injury on a piece of scrap metal. Which had resulted in a tetanus shot as well, and she was very glad to have what she needed on hand.

But her mind kept circling back to the fact that when she'd woken, Roades hadn't been on the sofa. Or anywhere else in the house.

She emptied the basin of water and blood down the drain and went through the disinfecting process. Scrubbing out the basin and then leaving it overturned to dry. Then she removed her gloves and scrubbed her hands with antibacterial soap.

The moves were familiar but the thoughts swirling through her head were not. Roades was gone, she was sure of it. She knew the difference of the lonely, empty house she shared with a cousin she didn't often cross paths with and when Roades was there. Just having him inside the four walls left the place feeling fuller.

And her life less empty.

She'd pushed him away, and he'd gone. It was the only conclusion she could come to.

The man hadn't even put up a fight! She hadn't even given a lot of effort to telling him to back off. Surely, if he was serious about her, he would have given some resistance.

That was the thing—he *wasn't* serious. He'd only come back into her life to help with Hernan out of some silly old guise of friendship. And she'd been beyond stupid to let her physical attraction and needs take over.

The place smelled of blood.

She walked to the door and threw it open and then went back inside, pushing up window sashes and finding one sticking. A step sounded behind her, and she threw a look over her shoulder, thinking it another patient since the boot-fall wasn't heavy enough to be Roades.

"Take a seat and I'll be with you in a moment. I'm just trying to get this window up and some air flowing through," she said.

"Is that how a sister greets a brother?"

She whirled to see Hernan there in the doorway, looking much worse for wear. With a cut on his forehead that looked tight and swollen. and with new lines on his face that revealed how tough the path he'd chosen really was, he hardly looked like the brother she knew.

A cry left her, and she ran across the space to throw her arms around him. Criminal or not, he was still her family and she loved him. She also hadn't given up on him, or she wouldn't have bothered calling Roades.

Roades. She wondered if Hernan had seen him yet.

She released him and stepped back, wrinkling her nose. "You smell."

He chuckled like the boy she'd always known. "I guess I do. Carissa, I can't stick around. I just hoped you'd look at this cut." He pushed his hair off his forehead to show the wound extending up to his hairline and looking angrier with each inch.

She gasped and pointed at the padded table. "Lie down."

He did without argument, which must mean he really was in pain. And no wonder—the cut was infected. She collected the supplies she'd need to tend him, all the time wondering where Roades was. Now would be the ideal time for him to show his face. He could give Hernan a lecture that would scare the

Jesus back into him and then be on his way back to Louisiana.

That would mean she'd never see him again, most likely. And she'd be forever wondering what he did for a living that had packed so much muscle on him. But that was neither here nor there — she didn't need to know those things.

I only want to.

She turned to Hernan. Brushing the hair back from his forehead made her think of the times she'd tucked him into bed when he was a boy. And the times she'd comforted him after their parents had died in the crash. How had she done so badly at teaching him to be a better man?

He met her gaze. "You look tired, 'Rissa."

She pushed out a sigh. She hadn't slept much the previous night, too busy listening for Roades and hoping he'd make an attempt to get into her bed again. But he hadn't and God knew where the man was now.

Irritation wove through her.

"I'm tired because I've been up worrying about my brother."

"Me?"

She cuffed him in the ear, and he rolled away. "Yes, you, *estupido niño!* What do you think you're doing, keeping people from fresh water? Charging them to get something they need to survive and you have no right to withhold!"

She moved to slap at him again, and he jumped off the table to his feet. He glared at her, and her heart tripped.

This was her worst fear — seeing Hernan turn into something she despised. It had finally happened.

He shook the hair off his forehead and stared her down. "You don't know anything about survival, do you, sister? You believe the world is all good, treating wounds and broken bones and getting paid in chicken eggs. Well, you could do nothing without my help, don't you realize that?"

She stepped back. She knew he and Angel were friends but hadn't realized his buddy could be trading with her because Hernan ordered him to. As if she hadn't felt seedy enough about the trades she made, now she felt even more disgusted.

She stiffened and met his gaze. "You don't need to worry about me, *hermano*. I can take care of what I need without your help."

He blanched at her use of the word 'brother' but a hard, cold look took over his face. "That's fine. You can stay out of my business as well, *hermana*."

Icy cold water splashed over her, but she could be just as hard as he was. Actually, tougher, if need be. Who had held it together after their parents' deaths? In the days since Hurricane Maria?

She pointed to the door. "You'd better find somebody to tend that cut on your forehead. It's festering."

He grunted and walked out, not bothering to look back or close the door.

Carissa picked up the stainless-steel bowl of gauze and disinfectant and threw it across the room. It crashed into the wall and landed on the floor with a clatter that echoed in her ears.

But it was nothing compared to the pain resounding in her heart. She had to find Roades and stop her brother.

Chapter Six

When Roades entered the clinic, the soft rasp of a heartbroken sob hit him like a blast. He stepped inside and closed the door, raking his gaze over the small, clean space for the source of that sound.

His heart slammed his chest wall so hard he could only hear his own pulse until he remembered his training and forced his heartrate to slow.

"Carissa?" He expected to see her crumpled in a corner, bruised and bloodied. Dammit, why had he left her alone to go out searching for Hernan?

The front of the clinic was for patients, set up with a bed, two chairs and a cabinet full of supplies, all painted in the same pristine white. But there was a small storage room.

In two steps he reached the storage doorway, looking at the floor first but only seeing Carissa's feet clad in leather sandals. His heart surged, and he jerked his gaze upward, drinking in the woman who from the back, appeared to be whole.

She was bent over a table filled with all sorts of produce and trinkets, her face in her hands as she cried her heart out.

Jesus, this woman had gotten right under his skin after only one day.

He stepped up to her and grabbed her shoulders. She jerked in his hold like a frightened bird, struggling until he said, "Carissa!"

Relief hit her features but it didn't help her red-rimmed eyes or tear-stained face.

He looked her over. How many times had he done this with people he protected? Too often Knight Ops was thrown into the middle of a situation involving bystanders or hostages—and then Ben often sent Roades to assess the situation.

"What happened?"

She shook her head, her face crumpling all over again.

"Are you hurt?" Icy dread hit his system at the thought of wounds he couldn't see. She didn't appear to be a rape victim, her clothes intact. But that didn't mean she hadn't cleaned herself up.

When she didn't immediately respond, he shook her lightly. "Did someone hurt you?"

She shook her head again, eyes clearing a bit at the urgency in his tone. "I'm okay, Roades."

He searched her face. "You don't sound okay. What's going on?"

"Hernan came to visit me."

Fucking.

Hell.

He'd gone out searching for the man and like an idiot, he'd left Carissa unprotected.

"He was hurt."

"I don't give a shit if he's hurt. I care about what he did to you."

She blinked at the vehemence in his voice. "He just said things. It was nothing, Roades."

He thumbed away a tear trickling down her cheek, making its way to the corner of her plump lips. "Doesn't look like nothing, *mon coeur*."

"He basically said that the things I need — the first-aid supplies and the drugs I've been... *trading* are only available to me because of him. And now he won't let me have those things."

Roades had liked Hernan from the start, but after just five minutes in the household, he'd realized Carissa and Hernan's parents were weak. They pampered their children and didn't like to rock boats, which had left Hernan running the show and Carissa battling to keep him in check. Hernan had been facing some trouble for theft, and Roades had stepped up for the kid and vouched that he would not do it again if charges were dropped.

The rest of the weeks Roades spent with the family, he'd made it a point to offer Hernan good words of advice and a wealth of influence when it came to how strength grew from moral fiber and not by using terror to get what he wanted. When he'd been forced away from Puerto Rico, he'd gone believing Hernan might grow to be a better man.

How wrong he was.

He cupped Carissa's face. She might have told him what had happened between them was a mistake, but he didn't give a fuck. It didn't feel that way to him, and he wasn't going to hold back from comforting her right now.

"Even after crying, you have the most beautiful eyes," he grated out.

A puff of air left her, and she raised her hands to cover his palms on her cheeks. "Roades, I said—"

"I know what you said." Against his will, he released her and stepped back. Gathering his thoughts again, he said, "So Hernan is basically blackmailing you."

"I don't know about blackmail..."

He stared at her. "You're fooling yourself if you believe otherwise. He wants you on his side and if you're not, then you don't get what you need for your clinic. It's emotional blackmail in exchange for goods."

She opened her mouth and snapped it shut again. She twisted to stare at the items on the table.

God, he hated being right, but he wasn't one to sugarcoat or blow smoke up asses. He was trained to walk in, assess a situation and say it plain. Or act. He planned to do both.

He touched her shoulder. "What is all this stuff?" He gestured to the goods, including a brass candleholder, some squash and a half dozen brown eggs in a tattered cardboard box.

"Payment," she said softly.

God, these people had regressed hundreds of years. They'd resorted to paying for services with whatever they could spare.

And Carissa was good enough to accept it.

She gathered up the eggs and turned. "Might as well cook lunch before someone comes in with a dislocated shoulder or some other injury. Are you hungry?"

Hell yeah, but not for what she was holding. He dipped his gaze to her breasts. When he glanced back up at her face, her warm tan skin bore a deeper hue on her cheeks and throat. Damn if he didn't want to kiss every bit of her.

He managed to control himself and resisted pinning her to the nearest wall. He even managed to hold open the door for her to pass through. Once again, his mind went straight to the security of this place.

Not only was she known by a gang and whatever unsavory people Hernan associated with, but she was sitting on a goldmine of narcotics. The flimsy walls of her clinic could easily be kicked in, the locks smashed off the storage cupboards. So why hadn't those things happened yet?

He wondered if Carissa had become an off-limits zone. He'd seen it in war—where a medic was spared because of the people he needed to save. Maybe that was the case with Carissa, but even so, Roades needed to up the security measures.

If Hernan had visited her, he'd also probably heard that Roades was in town. And he'd be avoiding Roades like the plague. Which meant Roades would need to be out of the house a lot, combing the dark alleys and abandoned spaces for the kid and leaving Carissa unprotected.

As soon as she stepped foot in the house, he moved ahead of her, circling the rooms, looking for anything out of the ordinary.

"What are you doing?" she asked.

"Making sure it's safe for you."

She eyed him. "But not for you?"

He shrugged, a cocky grin hitting his lips. "I can handle myself."

She set down the eggs on a counter next to the sink and faced him. "Isn't it time to tell me what you do?"

He arched a brow. "What I do? That could span a lot of territory. Lately, I fish a lot. You might recall how much I love catfishin'."

She folded her arms and nodded, but he knew she was only prompting him for more information faster. Her pose said *get to the point* but her rosebud lips remained sealed into a perfect line.

"I did some work around the house for my parents recently."

"I suppose that packed a lot of muscle on you."

"Sure."

"Roades." Warnings sounded in her voice.

"Are you askin' how I got the physique you see before you now?" He ran a hand up his abs, his shirt moving up to expose his six-pack to her.

Her gaze dropped to his waist and she wet her lips before looking back into his eyes. "I wouldn't put it that way, but yes."

Damn, the little beauty was playing hard to get now. Pretending she wasn't aching for him to get her into bed and her panties weren't already wet.

"I can't tell you what I do."

Her expression went from gleaming interest to lights-out in a blink. "Does that mean you're involved in criminal activity?"

He actually threw back his head and laughed for a long minute. When he looked back at her, she'd folded her arms more tightly and her posture was as closed as could be. But he knew one word, one step toward her, would have her right where he wanted her.

Unraveling for him.

"Carissa."

Her chest heaved. For a second, he thought he had her, but she stiffened again.

Whirling to the sink, she placed the eggs in the bottom and poured water from a jug over them, washing the shells. Her movements were jerky enough that he read her anger loud and clear.

She let out a string of Spanish under her breath. His language skills were impeccable but he couldn't make out everything she whispered.

He leaned against the counter next to her. "What was that about a dog's ass, *mon coeur*?"

She slanted a look at him. "I said you're as bright as one but you think you're smarter," she said, boldly meeting his stare.

He laughed again. Damn, he hadn't had this much fun in a long time. His job was stressful, and it was even more stressful to be away from it. Though the Knight Ops could deal with the homegrown terrorist bullshit right now—Roades was happy where he was.

"Will you please drop this act and tell me what you do? It's clear that you're aware of danger and know how to handle it. Don't you think I deserve to know who I'm dealing with?"

He cocked his head. "*Who* you're dealing with? You know damn well who I am."

"No, I don't. The young man I knew didn't wear frown lines between his eyebrows. He didn't look like he could kill someone with a jab of his pinky finger. And he wouldn't hide things from me."

That got him right by the heartstrings.

92

She was right that he'd been throwing up barricades between them. He had no fucking choice. He'd leave soon and return to his world, leaving her to…

He looked around.

This.

This house that seemed to lean to one side, probably shifted on its foundation by the storm's winds. And he'd be leaving her to defend herself. What if someone finally decided she wasn't off-limits and stole everything from her? She could lose it all.

She could lose her life.

He swallowed the burning ember of fear in his throat and watched as she put a cast iron skillet on the circa 1950s range. That she still had gas to run the stove was a wonder to him. There wasn't even electricity in the house.

She lit the burner and slammed the pan over it. Then she reached for a dish of butter and dropped a fat dollop in. It melted and sizzled. She cracked in the eggs—all six of them.

The scents made his stomach cramp with hunger, but he couldn't stop eyeing the arch of her throat, too aware of all the sensitive spots that would make her writhe for him and gasp out his name.

"Carissa."

She tossed him a look over her shoulder but went back to adding salt and pepper to the eggs along with a bit of pepper flakes for the heat he remembered in

93

Puerto Rican cooking. She'd probably also set out a jar of homemade hot sauce to douse the eggs in.

God, this place held so many memories for him. Good ones too. He'd lived an entire lifetime in that month spent here, and it had taken every year since to try to forget the love they'd shared.

"I work for the government."

She froze, the spatula she held dangling over the pan.

"For homeland security in a special ops force. That's all I can say on that front. But before that, I was a Marine, served a year in Afghanistan."

She whipped around to look at him, as if expecting to see a lie written over his face. When she saw it was the truth, she said, "Well, that accounts for the muscle."

He leaned close, his lips near her ear. "Does the muscle bother you? I thought yesterday that you approved. Liked it, even."

A shiver rolled through her, but she didn't turn into his arms as he hoped. Stubborn, beautiful woman.

"You liked seeing me undressed. Touching my body," he went on in a whisper.

She flipped two eggs at once and broke both. The yellow yolks seeped into the pan. She kept her profile to him but he didn't see her blink or even draw a breath.

94

"I loved touching yours. I'd like to taste you next time, *mon coeur*."

Her breath hitched and escaped in a rush. "Roades, I told you—"

He cut her off. "I know what your mouth said. But I can look into your eyes and see the truth there, Carissa. The desire."

She swallowed hard, her delicate throat working with the action. "Get me two plates off the shelf."

Satisfied that she wasn't as hardened to him as he feared, he reached up to pull down two plates, handmade pottery with swirls of color in the centers. She flipped the eggs onto the plates, two for herself and four for him, giving him both the broken ones. Which only amused him more. God, he'd missed her.

They sat at the table and she gave him some fresh water from the jug, though it was warm, and some crusty bread with a thick coating of butter to eat with the eggs.

Seated across the small table with her gave his heart a pang. If they'd continued together, gotten married… would this have taken place every single morning? Banter and sexual foreplay, a plate of eggs and a sassy Puerto Rican woman?

He was seriously beginning to reevaluate his life.

She used her fork to cut into an egg and place a section on the bread. He watched her take a bite and chew.

"If you're waiting for me to react to what you've told me, you will wait for a long time," she said.

"Why is that?" He took a bite of eggs. The freshness of everything was so much better than the crap he usually ate on the road with Knight Ops. His *maman's* Cajun homecookin' was another story. The sun rose and set on her jambalaya.

"I know your brothers were in the military back when we were together. I always wondered if that's why you left — to join up."

He paused mid-bite, fork in the air. "You think I left you to join the Marines?"

She lifted a slender shoulder in a half-shrug. "Makes sense. You were young. I was younger. I can't blame you for making choices that would mean the rest of your life."

He dropped his fork. It clattered to the plate and he leaned across the table. "Carissa, you meant the goddamn world to me."

She stared at him.

"Don't look at me that way, like you don't buy it. It's true." He picked up his fork again and ate an egg whole, not even tasting it.

"You always said you wouldn't follow in their footsteps, but I knew you were lying to me. Or yourself. Or both of us." She chewed a bite of bread, delicate jaw working.

He growled out his frustration. "I know I said that. I was young, Carissa. You were too. Let me ask

96

this—would you have become a nurse if we'd gone and gotten married? Or would you just have become my wife and the mother of my children?"

She took a moment to think on it then nodded slowly. "You're right. We're both better off now, and we serve our people in better ways than we would have together."

Ouch. Fucking hell, she knew how to gouge him in the soft spots.

They finished the meal in silence and then he stood and carried his plate to the sink. "Thank you for lunch. I'm going back out. Don't expect me back, and make sure you lock up."

She rose to a stand, deep brown eyes burning with something he couldn't understand. But he'd give anything to see her look at him the way she had when he laid her down on her bed the previous day.

She nodded. "Take care of yourself, Roades."

He made it to the door before he turned around. She was all soft curves and big eyes as he stomped back. Taking her face in between his hands, he crushed his mouth over hers. She didn't push him away or fight him off, only parted her lips for him to glide his tongue in—once.

He released her and went back to the door. "Don't think less of me because I can protect you like I always should have been able to." He opened the door and slammed it behind him.

* * * * *

Roades' Spanish was getting a workout. While he was fluent, he used more Cajun than anything, though it hadn't taken him long to think in the language as he searched for Hernan.

It crossed his mind that he hadn't asked Carissa if she knew where her brother had gone or the haunts he kept. Then again, he wouldn't have told Carissa anyway. Roades would have more luck finding him and when he did, well... that little punk better start saying his rosary now.

In Afghanistan, he'd walked the streets and spoken to the people. Doing so now felt familiar, and he felt his energy being boosted with each step he took. He stopped to tease a young mother juggling a baby and several bags, bringing a smile to her face. Then he stood on a corner shooting the breeze with a couple old men. Stooped, worn thin by the conditions they were living in but willing to joke about the things Roades touched on.

He saw a young woman coming out from between two buildings with a bundle tucked close to her chest. She threw a look over her shoulder before rushing up the street.

Roades zeroed in on the girl and then the alley. She was no older than Carissa and if he had his guess, she wasn't carrying her laundry.

She was no concern of his. He headed for the buildings.

98

There were a lot of places for Hernan to hide but if he was extorting money for goods, that meant he couldn't go too deeply underground. He needed access to people and they needed to find him without asking too many questions.

He jogged across the street and took a second to watch the pedestrians. If anyone made a move for the alley, he'd stop and interrogate him. He leaned against the building as if he was just soaking up the sun's rays and waited.

When a young boy popped out from between the buildings with a bundle similar to the girl's, Roades called out to him.

The kid froze. No more than ten, he shouldn't be sent on such errands. Then again, these kids weren't the pampered kids he knew, sitting on their couches playing video games.

"What is between those buildings, son?" he asked the boy in his language.

The kid looked skeptical about telling him, but Hernan and people like him would be moving around to keep the authorities off their trail—word of mouth was the only way to locate them.

"*Una puerta*," the child answered.

A door. Just as Roades suspected.

"Where does the door lead?"

The boy shifted uncomfortably from foot to foot. Then he stepped closer and parted the cloth of the bundle. Roades leaned in to peek, confirming his suspicions. A bottle of water, a packet of food and some pills in a small baggie.

"Who are the pills for? Not for you?" Some of them were opioids and if he found out this child was taking them…

He shook his head, dark hair flopping around his ears. "*No, señor. Mi padre.*"

Roades looked into his eyes. He'd seen addiction and the havoc it wreaked in families. And yes, the kid had shadows in his big brown eyes.

His very first commander's words came back to him. *You can't save the whole goddamn world.*

So following the boy back to his house and roughing up his father was out of the question.

He sighed. Guess he had to settle for stopping the opioid deals at the root.

He offered the boy a smile and reached into his pocket, pulling out a handful of hard candies and taffy. Good thing he had a sweet tooth. "These are for you. Best run on home quickly, boy."

The child's face lit and he opened the bundle to allow Roades to drop the candies in. Then he took off down the street quickly, heels kicking high.

"Fuck," Roades muttered and took off into the alley.

He was prepared for anything, willing to kill if he must. Knight Ops wasn't all running in and shooting 'em up. They calmed hostage situations and had even taken down a religious compound with a nut-job at the wheel. God, what a fucking mess that ended in. Body bags all over the damn place...

Parts of the building had been torn away, but not by winds. It looked as if someone had removed pieces to use someplace else. The door was about halfway down on the left, and he didn't stop to perform some secret knock if there was one.

He whipped it open, hand on his weapon.

Sweet Jesus, the room was stacked high with boxes. Like the last hidey-hole he'd raided times ten. His gaze landed on one of the crates he'd seen in Carissa's locked storage area, and anger hit him again. She shouldn't have to live this way, and the only thing that had kept him from confiscating all of her crates was the knowledge that she was using them for good. Wrong or not, she had made a choice and saving people's lives was it.

For a minute, nobody inside the space moved. Expecting him to say what he could give them for the things he needed, they didn't view him as a threat.

Until he pulled his weapon from behind his back.

Two men reacted by whipping their automatic weapons up and shouting for him to stand down. Roades nearly laughed—they probably believed him just a common thug out to steal from the big thieves. But they were fucking wrong.

He ran at them, catching them off guard. One squeezed off a round, and Roades slid under the spray, kicking the man's legs out from under him and snapping an ankle in the process. While the attacker writhed on the terra cotta tile, Roades grabbed his weapon and turned to the second man, who was bearing down on him so Roades stared up the barrel of his weapon.

He gave the guy, nineteen at most if Roades was to guess, a grin. "I'm looking for Hernan."

"Hernan's not here," he spat back.

"But he's in charge here." Roades was slowly moving his pistol hand forward, lining up with the man's foot as he used conversation to distract. It was his experience that most men couldn't think and fight, and he was confident this dead-behind-the-eyes man wouldn't prove him wrong.

"Who are you coming here asking questions? Fucking *extranjero*." The word meaning outsider didn't faze Roades.

He took the shot. The shock on the man's face as his foot exploded into several pieces was mild compared to his determined rage. He went to shoot Roades, but Roades was bigger, stronger and readier. He leaped up, elbowing the man square in the nose. A satisfying crunching sound as well as the shots had other men running into the room.

Shouts sounded. In his pocket, his phone buzzed with an incoming call. It could be Carissa, but he wasn't in a position to answer it right now. He was sorta busy.

He surged forward, aiming to take down but not kill. He kneed one guy in the balls and flipped him over his shoulder, then stepped on his fingers, crunching them around the weapon so he could no longer shoot.

Another guy thought to catch him while his hands were full, but Roades smashed his pistol across the asshole's face and when he stumbled, Roades put a shoulder beneath him, lifting and heaving him into a wall.

"Anybody else want a piece of this? Trust me, it won't be pretty," he called out. When nobody took him up on his offer, he said, "I'm looking for Hernan."

A younger male had plastered himself to the wall as if to blend in with what appeared to have once been a beautiful mural of the harbor. "He's not here," the kid said in a faltering voice. By Roades' guess, he had wet pants.

Roades braced his legs wide. "But he was."

The kid nodded.

"When will he be back?"

"He doesn't tell us. We just do the business while he's gone."

Roades pointed to the men lying around, some whimpering in agony. The kid blanched. "Make sure Hernan sees this. If he doesn't return in time, you send him pictures. Understand?"

He gave a hasty nod. Roades walked over to the boxes and looked inside several. There was everything from flour to a silver tea set, obviously traded for necessities. Jesus, this was the worst possible situation as far as Roades could see. He was certain now that he couldn't talk Hernan out of being this dictator over the town. This wasn't some naïve kid with weak parenting that he was dealing with. He couldn't even promise Carissa he wouldn't kill him, because if it meant Roades' life—or hers—Hernan would die.

He took the crate of narcotics and tucked it under his arm. "This is my trade for letting you all live."

Walking out into the sunshine after that was a shock. The rich scents of frying meat from a street vendor reached him, and the normalcy washed away the blood and echoes of bullets in his ears.

He quickly walked to the end of the alley and into the street. Zigzagging into crowds in case anybody was following him and sure they weren't, but his training wouldn't allow him to casually walk away from a fight like that and not believe there would be revenge.

As he made his way back to Carissa's clinic with the crate, he put some quick in his step. Also, someone had called him during the tussle. He took out his phone and saw the unfamiliar number that wasn't Carissa but an unknown which could only be the Knight Ops team.

He couldn't speak out here in the open and humped it faster to reach the clinic. When he found the door locked, he went to the house. The spice of cooking food, dinner, was in the air, and he realized how long he'd been out on the streets searching for Hernan. He walked farther into the house.

"Carissa?" He pushed open the bedroom door and stopped dead at the sight of her, shapely leg poised to slide into some loose black pants she held. Freshly washed, her dark hair wet around her shoulders and trailing to her black bra.

Fucking hell.

She looked up, surprise flitting over her pretty face, followed by something else. Then she directed her stare to what he held.

"Where did you get that?"

"Earned it."

She slipped her toes into the pants and then the other foot. When she drew the fabric over her hips, he had the insane thought that she was sexier clothed than not. His chest burned, and he realized he was holding his breath.

Turning her back on him, she donned a tank top before facing him again. "Earned it how? With your fists?" She dropped her gaze to his knuckles, which were splattered with blood.

He shrugged. "Give me the keys to your clinic and the storage room and I'll lock it up."

She breezed past him as if she encountered special forces in her bedroom every day of her life. She opened a box on her nightstand and drew out a set of keys. She tossed them to him, and he snagged them from the air.

It took everything in him not to drop the crate and take her in his arms. The bed was alluringly close, and it had been several hours since he'd tasted her. That one little kiss had done nothing to satiate the extreme craving for her.

As he went out to the clinic, he battled to find his wits. Besides a dozen ways to make Carissa scream with pleasure, one major thing was on his mind—he couldn't stick around here because Hernan would come looking for him, and there was no way in hell Roades was bringing that to Carissa's doorstep. Also, he needed to call his brother and see what was happening.

After replacing the crate in the clinic and locking everything, he paced the small yard and made the call.

"Didn't know if you'd call back," Ben drawled into his ear.

"What's happening?" Roades asked. In the background, the noise of a celebration sounded. Music, the clink of beer bottles. "You at a bar?"

"Nah, out at the cabin."

Nostalgia and severe homesickness swept Roades. He was far from the bayou and the family

106

cabin there. The place he thought of as a safe haven, a place he'd gone several times between missions to get his shit together after things he'd seen or done.

His eyes cleared and he stared at his true surroundings — the storm-weathered house, a shaft of sunlight on the yard and the plants Carissa had potted. He touched one and it released a medicinal scent. Must be some herb she used for her clinic.

"Tell me what's been happening," Roades said.

"I can't disclose much, and especially over the phone. But we took some heavy blasts and we're all lucky as fuck to be alive." Ben didn't sound very concerned about anything but celebrating their lives, and Roades couldn't blame him.

He should fucking be there with them though, dammit.

He shoved his fingers through his hair and stared at the small window to the house. It sat over the kitchen sink, where earlier Carissa had washed the eggs for their lunch. He was fucking worlds away from where he needed to be, and yet he didn't want to leave either.

A cheer went up in the background, coupled with a splash that could only mean one of the guys had gotten shoved off the dock into the bayou. Ben chuckled. "We miss the fuck outta you, bro."

Roades' chest was tight. "When am I being reinstated?"

"Dunno. Jackson's being a prick, as always."

"Well, he's your father-in-law. Can't you pull some strings for me?"

"Where the hell are you, anyway? *Maman* said you hadn't been home in a few days. You holed up with that little redhead you were seein'?"

Roades had to shake his head to even figure out what the hell Ben was talking about. All he could see was a dark-haired beauty, soap and water fresh.

"Nah, man. I'm in Puerto Rico."

A beat of silence. "What are you doin' there? Cohen mentioned he'd seen you. He fly you down, bro?"

Roades probably shouldn't have said anything to Ben. His brother wasn't one for gossip, but he wouldn't keep any information about Roades from the Knight Ops team — or their family.

"Yeah, he did. I'm takin' *Maman's* advice and doing something that isn't focused on me." Like playing with a pair of beautiful breasts, if he had his way.

Ben laughed. "Well, she'll be proud. We did miss you, man. You shoulda been there with us. I'm sorry as hell that you're in this position, but I think you could do some good down there after the hurricane."

"Me too," he said quietly.

They ended the call after a few more words, leaving Roades standing alone in a yard in a foreign land, feeling about as lost as a man could.

Then Carissa came to the back door and everything came crashing back at him. Carissa, his reason for being here — and yeah, it was much bigger than himself.

* * * * *

"Are you injured?" Carissa's question didn't only extend to the blood on Roades' knuckles. She could see by his face something was wrong.

She dropped her gaze to the phone in his hand. "You got a call out?"

He gave a rough nod. "My brother."

"Is everything all right?" She stepped up to him, tipping her head to meet his stare.

After a second, his eyes cleared. "Yeah, it's all good."

"Doesn't sound so convincing. What about these? Is this your blood or not?" She took his hands.

"Not."

She shouldn't be shocked, yet she couldn't help but be. The man before her was trained to kill — had he? Wouldn't he be covered in more blood than a few specks if that was the case?

"Come inside and wash it off then. I've fixed dinner."

"I told you not to expect me back."

She snorted. "You aren't the only person who gets hungry, you know."

He gave a huff of amusement and followed her back into the house. She was aware of his heated stare on her as she moved through the rooms she'd tidied to keep her hands busy today and went into the kitchen.

She went to the sink and plucked up a bar of soap, holding it out to him. He nudged her aside and used the clean water from the jug to scrub up. "When do they hope to fix the water supply so it isn't tainted?" he asked.

She couldn't pull her gaze from his hands as he lathered, the veins and tendons giving her visions of other ways he could use his hands. Her pussy pulsated at the memory of his fingers buried there.

He was looking at her, and she realized she hadn't answered his question.

"Oh. No word. They just say to keep getting the fresh water."

"Ah." He rinsed and dried with a clean towel. He turned from the sink. "Dinner smells fantastic. Asopao?"

She smiled. "I didn't think you'd remember that dish."

"How could I forget? Your mother's specialty."

"And you said it's similar to your *maman's* gumbo."

"You can still use the Cajun." He smiled at her accent.

Feeling a warmth deeper than the heat of the day or his rugged presence, she pointed to a chair. "Sit and let me get you a plate."

Having the big man in her house gave her a sense of peace. She didn't love being totally alone, and that had been her lot in life the past few years since Hernan had gone his own way. And if she was honest, she was glad to know Roades was safe.

She spooned the thick rice, shellfish and chorizo onto the plates and carried them to the table. She paused. He dwarfed her furniture and looked like a grown man seated at a child's table for pretend tea.

He smiled at her, a light back in his eyes that had been absent when she'd found him in the garden. Her heart gave a little bleep of excitement and she took her seat.

"It looks as good as it smells." He placed his hands on the table, giving her a chance to admire those long fingers, now clean.

She wanted to ask what had happened to put the blood on his hands, but she didn't want to seem she was attacking him either. She wasn't going to preach pacifism to a man who did the job Roades did. There was a time for taking care of business, and if he hadn't been in that alley with her, God knew what her fate would have been. But she couldn't help but wonder if that blood was her brother's.

She was torn, and there was no remedying that. So she asked him another question.

"Did your brother say something to upset you?"

His chest expanded to what seemed to be an impossible size, and then he blew out his breath. "They are just back from a mission." His jaw clamped on the words and he picked up his spoon.

"They are special forces as well?"

He met her gaze. "I guess you wouldn't know because I didn't tell you. I always assume because... well, it feels like I've known you forever."

She nodded, not wanting to feel the old butterflies of love taking flight in her stomach, and yet they were flying around in a mad swirl.

He went on, "My unit, it's made up of me and my four brothers and one other guy."

Her brows rose. "All five of you?"

"Yeah. And I hate like hell that they face this shit without me. I should be there." He shoveled in a bite and chewed.

"Did your brother call because someone was hurt?"

He shook his head. "Thank God, no. But I guess it was close."

She didn't want to pry and ask why he wasn't there with them. Either he'd share the reason in his own time or he wouldn't.

He held up his spoon with spiced broth and chicken on it. "You make this dish better than your mother."

She laughed. "She would be proud then, but I think you're just flattering me."

He lowered the spoon to the plate and stared at her in a way that had her stomach fluttering all over again. His eyes grew soft and the pulse in his neck hammered fast.

"Carissa, *mon coeur*, there's so much to flatter about you."

The endearment would never get old if he said it hourly until she was a hundred. She hadn't touched her meal, because she couldn't stop thinking about taking him to her bedroom and doing unspeakable things to that brawny body of his.

Their past, their chemistry, it all ripped away anything her brain was telling her about dealing with Roades.

He set down his spoon and reached a hand across the table to her.

And damn if she didn't take it.

She didn't remember getting to the bedroom— only his kisses once he swept her up in his strong arms. The feel of being wrapped tight against him and his mouth slanting over hers made her weak.

Clinging to his shirt front, she stroked her tongue against his, gathering groans from him. Passion spread through her until she couldn't have stopped if another category five hurricane hit.

113

He skimmed his hands down her torso, grazing the sides of her breasts. When they landed on her hips and he tugged her against his hard cock, she gasped.

"I need to taste you," he grated out. "Then I'm going to slide my cock into your pussy and stretch you so good."

She yanked at his shirt, and he broke free of the cotton with a move of his arms like an untamed beast. God, this man was so beautiful, so wild. The violence he was capable of didn't frighten her at all, if she was honest, because she knew it would never be directed at her. No, he had only tenderness for her.

She coursed her palms up his chest, over his hardened nipples. He flicked a bad-boy grin her way, so she did it again, running her hands back down over them to his chiseled abs—and lower to his waistband.

When she dipped her fingers into his boxers, she met the spongy tip of his swollen shaft. He growled and turned her to the bed, rolling her down to the mattress and simultaneously pulling off her tank top.

The bra followed, and he sucked one nipple into his mouth while seeking to touch more of her. As he one-handedly shimmied down her loose gauzy pants, her hips rose and fell on their own, the tight band of need across her groin growing to an unbearable ache.

He lifted his head long enough to shoot her another smile she felt all the way to her curled toes. He pressed a kiss to her breast below her nipple. Then one directly below it. He continued a path, placing each little kiss in a perfect line over her ribcage and to her hipbone.

He swirled his tongue in the hollow there. Liquid heat hit her pussy, and she bucked upward without willing her body to move. Then he cut across to her mound. Stretching out between her legs, he thumbed apart her pussy lips. The wash of warm breath over her exposed, wet folds made her cry out.

She couldn't even find a single word in her head to beg him to lick her. So she tangled her fingers in his hair and guided him down.

The first brush of his lips over her sensitive folds had her twisting the sheets in her fists. He opened his mouth over her pussy and glided his tongue up her seam, very slowly. So slowly that she could count the seconds that she didn't breathe. When he reached the top and her stiff clit, she rocked upward with a cry.

"Roades!"

"Mmm." He planted his hands on her hips and drew her up and into his face again and again, his tongue working magic up and down her slit even as the rhythmic brush of her pussy against his face drew more pleasure from her. A million nerve endings blazed to life. Her first orgasm was so close, just within reach. She could see it in her mind's eye, a burning ember she wanted to wrap both hands and her entire body around to see if she got scorched.

While sucking and teasing her clit, he eased two fingers down her pussy to her soaking entrance. He tormented the edge of the opening, drawing circles around and around it until she thought she'd die of desire.

His eyes were dark with wanting too, and he held her gaze captive as he slid those fingers home.

Deep.

Angled upward against her inner wall and stroking her G-spot. Pressing on it now as he sucked hard, taking control of her body like never before. She flooded him with juices and tossed her head on the pillow, unable to do anything but feel.

A spear of sensation hit her groin, and a heavy throb of her inner walls had her clamping around his digits. He groaned against her, and she pushed down on him, taking his fingers as deep as possible as the orgasm ripped through her.

Her body unraveled for him in hard jerks of her hips and loud cries. Before the final tremor left her, he was back at it, licking, his fingers pumping fast in and out of her body, over that one spot. That pleasure center that, at this moment, totally belonged to Roades.

* * * * *

How many nights had Roades fantasized about Carissa since leaving her? He wasn't about to look away from her beautiful face now. Lips curled into a satisfied smile of pleasure, a dusky glow over her cheekbones. Right now, the only thing that would make him tear his gaze from her would be the click of a weapon at the back of his head.

Even then, he wouldn't pull his fingers free of her tight, wet channel.

She thrashed on his hand, and he pressed deeper. When her walls started to pulsate, he zeroed in on her eyes. Her stare burned into him, and damn if his heart didn't react, feeling like he'd just hit that high. The same high he got leaping out of planes or taking his Ninja at high speed on the back roads of the bayou.

Dammit, this was even more dangerous. Carissa had been his first and he'd gone hunting for other things to give him that same rush of emotion, but now he had her back and his fingers buried deep in her.

A shuddering moan left her. Followed by a squeak. She was climbing toward orgasm, her body focused inward. At the moment she shattered, his own cock couldn't be any fucking harder. He was like a teenager hell-bent on getting the cheerleader's panties off, not the man who'd honed so much control over the past few years.

She cried out, rising and falling against the plunges of his fingers. He leaned over her and took her mouth in a searing kiss, tasting all the passion and need still boiling inside her.

When he drew his fingers slowly from her still-pulsating pussy, she gasped and threw her arms around him. Pulling him down so his weight flattened her. But she didn't seem to mind. He braced himself on his elbows and kissed her long and deep, extending the burn of need, wanting it to last forever yet impatient to thrust into her and find his own heaven.

Chest heaving, he drew back to stare down at her. Perfectly mussed, her dark hair strewn across the pillows and her skin all dewy. She was his same Carissa but different at the same time, and it was so much… more this time around.

Now he was getting all sappy when he should be balls-deep. What was he waiting for? Her liquid heat still wet his fingers and he was mad to get inside her.

But the moment stretched on.

She traced a fingertip over his biceps, over the American flag rippling there to a tree with roots that reached toward his elbow. "What is the tree?"

"Family," he grated out.

She swallowed and nodded. The one thing that had split them up. Looking back, he knew his parents had made the right decision for a son who was too young to be married, but how would they react now?

When he raised a hand to stroke the hair off her damp forehead, it had a touch of a tremor. "*Mon coeur*, you make me stop and think."

She nodded. "I know. Me too."

He rushed on before the words dried up. "About what would have been between us."

"We were young. Things happen for a reason."

"Like I was supposed to be trained to come back here and help you."

She nodded. Then pushed her pussy against his thigh. "And fuck me. If you ever get around to it."

A chuckle rose to his lips, and he rolled off the bed. Stripping for a beautiful woman could be one hell of a turn-on. He knew what his body looked like and how it attracted the opposite sex. But seeing the appreciation in Carissa's eyes meant so much more.

He dropped his jeans and stepped out of them. Then stroked his cock through his boxers, pulling the cotton around the bulge. She moaned.

"Take them off and let me taste you." Her words were a hot plea.

His balls drew up tight to his body and his cock throbbed. Need was close to exploding out of him, and he had to get a goddamn grip or he *would* be that teen boy again.

Stepping up to the bed, he slid his boxers down his hips. His cock sprang free. Carissa turned onto one side and gripped it at the base, wrapping those warm little fingers around the girth.

He threw his head back on a growl.

She trailed a fingertip over a vein, following it up to the tip and then swirling through the precum there. She flashed a look at him before parting her lips and taking him in her mouth.

Pleasure twisted with desire so great it bordered on pain. But still, he couldn't pull out of her hot, tempting mouth. The sparks threatening impending release shot through his abs, but still he didn't draw back.

He pushed his cock deeper.

Seeing the bulge of his head riding along the inside of her cheek and the way her eyes darkened—

"Enough." He jerked his hips back and before the coo of disappointment was fully past her lips, he pinned her to the bed. Nudging her thighs apart, he settled between them. With her scorching heat just a whisper away from his cock, his brain took that moment to wake up to reality.

"I forgot a condom. Unless you tell me you're on the pill."

Her eyes cleared a bit of the passion there. "No... I gave all the birth control I had in stock to the local teenagers."

He nodded. Leave it to Carissa to think about keeping more unwanted children from being born into this disaster zone, but that left Roades frustrated and rolling back to his feet to grab a condom.

"I only have a couple more of these. I'll have to track down some back alley supplier." He flashed a grin that she returned. When he flattened her to the bed again, she wrapped her thighs around him and held onto his shoulders. Her lips begging for kiss after kiss.

He lowered his head, willing to make the sacrifice. As he teased her with small nibbles that were almost playful in nature, his body refused to follow suit—he wanted her *now*. He slammed into her.

She cried out and latched onto him tighter. He took a moment to groan out a curse or two and then started to move. Withdrawing slowly and slamming home again. Deeper this time, the tip of his cock stroking a place that made her cry out.

He stared down at her, and she turned her face to bite his shoulder. He grunted at the pain and twitched his hips again. She dug her fingers into the sinew of his hips and ran her calves down the backs of his thighs.

With a quick flip, he had her on top, straddling him. She threw him a smile. Dark waves fell across her breasts, and he smoothed a tendril aside to strum the hard brown nipple tensed for him.

"I have better access this way." He closed his hands over both breasts, and she dropped her head back, rising and falling on his cock. Her rhythm slow and then suddenly growing frantic.

She peaked a third time, and the tightening of her pussy around his cock nearly had him shooting for the stars himself. Only reciting the alphabet in Greek—backward—held him off.

She hung forward, hair dangling around them. "That was a surprise."

"Came out of nowhere, did it? It's because you're primed for me, *mon coeur*." He drew her down to kiss her, cupping her face and one hand planted on her ass. He bucked his hips up once, filling her completely again.

Her mouth opened on a silent scream of pleasure. He plunged his tongue inside, sweeping the hot depths even as he fucked her. Hard. Fast. Slow. He wanted every way possible.

But he was quickly losing his firm grip on control. Each small rasp of pleasure from her set him more off balance until his hips couldn't keep a solid rhythm and he couldn't hold it together.

He slid his hand between them, firmly pressing down on her clit as he gnashed his teeth to withstand the explosion about to take place.

She settled her thighs farther apart on the bed, sliding down him another fraction. The rumble that turned into a growl that expanded into a roar rocked him. He squeezed his eyes shut on the sensation of a release so big that he'd have empty balls for days.

Till Carissa swayed her little round backside into sight again.

She continued to ride through his orgasm. When she planted her hands on his chest and sat back with a satisfied smirk on her pretty face, he laughed.

"Lookin' mighty smug," he grated out.

"Mm."

He still had his thumb over her clit and gave it a test rub. She squeezed him with her inner muscles. A fierce protectiveness threw him. He stared up at her, his thumb still moving on its own, back and forth over the straining button that was slick with arousal.

He drew her up and off his cock, dealt quickly with his condom and then rolled her into the covers and replaced his thumb with his lips over her button. Tasting her a second time had him throbbing once again, but harder to figure out was the ache spreading in his chest.

Bracketing her hips with his hands, he held her firmly as he tongued her slick seam, up and down, over her clit and back to her channel. She couldn't hold still, and he felt her building to a massive climax.

Just as it hit out of nowhere, he closed his eyes and lapped at her juices. Realizing his fucking heart was so deep in this woman that he was actually disappointed not to be lying here with a goal of making babies with her.

Fuck, he was in so much trouble.

Chapter Seven

The sun was barely edging over the horizon when Roades beat up his first thug of the day and left him lying in the street. As he spat out a glob of blood from the asshole getting in a lucky punch, he walked away. Wondering what the fuck he was going to do about leaving once his three months of probation was up.

Leaving Carissa behind in a place like this was out of the question. But he couldn't very well set her up in Louisiana when he was hardly there himself. Leaving her friendless, without family support of even Mari.

Maybe Mari could come too.

He shook his head. What the hell was he thinking? He and Carissa came from two separate universes. Only when they were together, it felt like one.

If only…

His thought was cut short by the vibration of his cell. When he picked up, the line was empty air, the connection lost. He turned a corner and checked his reception again just as it rang a second time.

He brought the cell to his ear. "Knight."

"It's Ben."

"What's wrong?" Roades and all his brothers and sisters had a sixth sense about the others. All these dark morning hours he'd been combing the streets for Hernan, his mind kept rotating back to his family.

"You're right there's something up, man."

"Fucking tell me." He stopped walking, keeping an eye around him for danger. Nobody out at this time of day was up to any good.

"Lexi's gone."

The air whooshed from him. He'd been waiting to hear anything but that. Their little sister who was more vulnerable owing to a rough birth that left her with a lack of oxygen for a spell, making her more naïve and more than a little susceptible to bad decision-making.

"What the fuck? I leave the country for a few days and you lose our sister?" Roades' throat was tight on a roar of frustration.

"*Maman* realized she hadn't come home last night, and when she went into Lexi's room, there was a note."

"Jesus." He slammed his fingers through his hair.

"It says she went out to explore herself."

"What the fuck does that mean?"

"Who the hell knows. It's Lexi."

"Goddammit. Why weren't you guys keeping a better eye on her?" He'd expect their sister Tyler to pull something like this. Not sweet little Lexi.

A notion hit him. "Where's Rocko?" The sixth man on their team had been eyeing up their sister when she was around. Plus, the guy seemed to know a lot about her. Claimed they talked sometimes when he attended the family gatherings, but Roades had his own ideas about what was going down.

"He's right here, man. Believe me, we thought of that too and we fucking drilled him like he'd been hiding a terrorist. Rocko doesn't know where she is any more than we do. All he could tell us was that she'd been doing some soul-searching."

"What the fuck does that mean?" Roades asked a second time.

"Again, who the hell knows. It's Lexi."

"Jesus Christ. I'm coming home and we'll track her down."

"Before you jump on the first aircraft outta San Juan, stop and think."

"I am thinking—that our baby sister's missing, probably out hitchhiking and offering strange men access to her bank card." Now he was riling himself more.

"Calm your balls there, Roades. Lexi's got some skills to get her by. I'm not saying we shouldn't go find her, and I'm going to do my best to do that. But I don't want you rushing home just yet. Why the hell are you there in the first place?"

Roades snapped his mouth shut, looking into the streets that were growing lighter by the minute, shapes emerging from the charcoal shadows now. Across the street were many boxes lined up along a building, and the rags protruding from the openings could only mean homeless families resided there.

He twisted his lips. "I'm doing some work."

"Work? Are you a merc now? Getting paid for hunting people down?"

"Not paid."

"But you are hunting somebody."

He considered his words, but there was no way around it. "Yeah."

A beat of silence. Then, "Are you with Carissa?"

"Yes," he said at once and realized it was a relief to share that information with his brother.

"Hell, Roades."

"She isn't the reason I'm here, but..." He could still smell her on him, that light spice of her perfume and the pleasure she'd spent at his hands, lips, cock. He'd left her sleeping and that image would be forever engraved on his brain.

"But she's quickly becoming a reason for me to stay."

The statement fell between them.

Ben pushed out a breath into the phone. "Fuck. When you were seventeen, I was in agreement with our parents, believing it was a good idea to separate you and Carissa because you were so young. But you aren't seventeen anymore, and nothing can stop you

127

from being with her. Except this is a hard life, man. Your life carries a lot of danger. Is she cut out for that?"

He scrubbed a hand over his face, feeling the lack of sleep but more than that, the lack of common sense. He'd dragged Carissa into his world, but what now? Leave her a second time, walk away and never look back?

The flip side of that was taking her with him, drawing her into his world of missions and secrets, of not knowing his whereabouts for weeks at a time. Hell, she was going crazy not knowing where Hernan was, so how would she handle that? When Roades had told her what he did for a living, she had been far from happy.

Would she be able to navigate this bumpy road of life with him? Now that Ben had asked the question, Roades was leaning toward the no end of the spectrum.

What was best for her was to quickly find Hernan and get the hell out of Puerto Rico. Let Carissa find a life for herself and fulfill his hopes for her happiness.

But that would be without him, and that didn't set well one... fucking... bit. Especially when he knew without a goddamn doubt that a man would be in her future. She was too beautiful, too sensual, too desirable to be alone for long.

"Roades, you still there? The line cracked."

"Yeah, I'm here. What are you doing about finding Lexi?"

"As much as we can. Knight Ops is on standby. Somethin' brewing in fucking Mississippi again."

"Jesus. I swear that one county breeds assholes." Roades was glad to be off the topic of Carissa, though it weighed on his mind like a tank. "Okay, so who goes after Lexi then?"

"Elise has recruited Bo."

Sean's wife's ties with her ex seemed to have no bounds if she was recruiting him to find their little sister. But Bo *was* special forces, and one of the best.

"He's willing to do it?" Roades asked.

"Says he is."

"As long as the fucker keeps his distance once he finds her."

Ben didn't miss a beat. "Already busted his balls on that. Lexi's too pretty for her own good, and she does favor those Daisy Dukes."

That brought a growl from Roades.

"Believe me, bro, I know it. All right, I've taken enough of your time and you've got a job to do there. Keep me posted and if you need transport, I'll have it there for you."

"Thanks. You keep me updated on the Lexi situation. Kiss *maman* for me. And you guys... guts and glory."

The motto hung in the silence between them.

"Will do," Ben said and ended the call.

Leaving Roades standing on a street in a foreign land wondering what the hell he was doing with his life. Letting down his team, his family, and having no damn clue what to do about Carissa.

* * * * *

Carissa had debrided the dead tissue out of a man's abscessed toe, set a broken wrist and bound it the best she could with the supplies on hand, taken care of countless cases of the flu going around and even helped a sick puppy by hydrating it.

Her past two days had seen a steady stream of patients walking into her clinic. But she hadn't set eyes on Roades once.

He'd climbed from her bed sometime during the night and she was still beating herself up over that slip-up. Landing in his bed one time was bad enough but he kept pulling her in, and she had to get her head on straight. She was far from the naïve, sheltered girl who'd fallen for the handsome, worldly young mainlander while staying with her aunt.

She was smart enough to know when things wouldn't work out, and this was one of those times. The sooner he found Hernan and put a stop to his crimes, the sooner Roades could go home.

Out of her life.

After washing with fresh heated water out of the big basin, she proceeded to dump the water into the back garden. At least her herbs were thriving, even if her heart was withering.

With nothing left to do, Carissa made herself a sandwich of tomato on toasted bread and a bowl of berries she'd gotten from a patient. Then she sat at the table, thinking of the huge Marine who'd sat across from her at this very table, giving her those bedroom eyes.

Right before rocking her world.

She pushed out a sigh and forced herself to eat though she wasn't very hungry. He was either on a hot trail or avoiding her. After seeing him in action, she wasn't even entertaining that he might be lying somewhere hurt. The man could walk away from an air strike.

The tomato was vibrant in her mouth, salted and delicious, but she ate mechanically. What she wouldn't give to have her mother here now, someone to confide in. Mari was on night shifts, and Carissa had been missing her, too busy with her clinic to visit during the days. Not that Mari's opinion of Roades was something Carissa wanted to hear again. She had freely offered it after Roades had left her at the altar, and she couldn't make her a confidante now.

Carissa had feelings for the man, that was undeniable. But she wasn't about to admit how deep they ran. The sex was the hottest, most amazing of her life, but she didn't need to tie her feelings to it, did she?

She wished she was worldlier, one of those women who could sleep with a man, take what pleasure she could and dump the rest. In Carissa's case, that wasn't possible, which was why she needed to stop sleeping with him pronto.

Who was she kidding? If he walked through that door right now, she'd ditch her boring tomato sandwich for a lick at that man-lollipop. Gliding her tongue down the ridges of his hard abs all the way to —

She shut off that thought and got up to throw away her sandwich. This wasn't healthy, to be dwelling on a man who'd walked away from her once and was destined to again. She had to put a stop to these ideas. Part of her wished she'd never called him.

But it had been so good to see him. To smell his scent and touch him. Looking into his dark eyes had been the highlight of her past five years.

Yeah, she needed to do something — now. She grabbed her cell, which was likely to be useless but she pocketed it nonetheless, along with a few bucks in cash. She locked the house and slipped out into the dying light of the day.

The heat had dissipated, leaving a cooler breeze that toyed with her hair as she walked down the street. Heading to the town, she mentally searched for her brother. Finding him was the first step to getting Roades to leave — and getting her life back. Her focus on the sexy special ops guy was bordering on obsessive.

Or love.

She pushed a sigh out of her burning lungs. She did love him, had never stopped. Now he was larger than life and like a wave during a hurricane, easy to be sucked into. If she wasn't swimming fast for shore, she'd never surface.

She walked to one of the places she often met Angel, but it was abandoned. The man hadn't come looking to trade supplies for crates of narcotics recently, and that was fishy as hell.

An image of that blood on Roades' knuckles popped to mind, and not for the first time, Carissa pondered if Angel had come to a reckoning with her ex-fiancé.

If she was honest, she'd admit how good it was to have him here, someone to look to for support. She'd been on her own so long, and since the disaster, the weight felt too heavy at times.

She left the alley and headed through the marketplace. The stalls were all closed up for the night, but the scents of fruits from the nearby orchards lingered even after they were packed away. At least her island still had some resources that Hernan couldn't lord himself over.

As a teen when Hernan had discovered the most trouble, he'd often hung out in one section of the city. *La Uniformada* hadn't even patrolled this part because they knew gangs ran rampant and they seemed to have given up the fight over turf and possessions. Too often the news would report a shooting there and

Carissa and her parents would be terrified one of the bodies would be Hernan's.

Then somehow, Roades had straightened that all out for a few years. What was said Carissa would never know but Hernan had accepted Roades' role as leader and followed by example, even in the very short time the man was in their lives.

She turned at one of the last stalls of the market, which smelled like fish, and walked down a cobbled road, her soft-soled shoes silent on the stones. She didn't need much light to know where she was going — she'd come looking for Hernan a few times in the past. But she was still unnerved. Why hadn't she thought to bring a flashlight?

Roades would kick her ass if he knew what she was doing, but it wasn't his call, was it? Throwing her shoulders back, she approached one of the storefronts that wasn't abandoned. Inside, she heard the strains of laughter and the clink of glasses that meant alcohol was being poured. And Puerto Ricans loved their music, so it was blasting through the cracks of the door.

When she opened the door, a huge man standing as bouncer looked down at her. His black hair fell in a greasy wave over his eye, and many women would find him dashing with all the muscles filling out his white shirt. But Carissa had seen a true god in Roades and her head wouldn't be easily turned.

She gave him a nod of greeting and started past him. He caught her arm. She threw him a smile over her shoulder, hoping to convince him to let her pass.

"This might not be a good place for you to be." His warning came off as more of a threat, but she was made of tougher stuff.

She arched a brow. "I know what I'm doing."

A grin stretched over his face and then he released her arm. She drew away and continued into the space, through groups of people clustered at tables with too many chairs pulled up to them or seating groups of leather couches. On a stage, a band had set up, and Carissa felt like she might be back in old times—mere weeks ago but it felt like forever—before Hurricane Maria had stripped so much from her people.

She craned her neck to see around dancing bodies, searching for the darkest corner of the club. Because that was where her brother would be, if he was here. If not him, then somebody who knew him.

She skirted four guys at a table. As she passed, something brushed her backside.

She whirled to see a man eyeing her, his hand outstretched.

He waggled his fingers at her.

Why he'd single her out of this crowd was beyond her. There were so many more beautiful women dressed provocatively, and she only had on a simple pair of jeans and a tank top. Men like this didn't care, though. They were looking for one thing — sex and power.

She continued on, ignoring him.

The scrape of a chair had the hair on her neck rising, and she glanced back in time to see the man on his feet.

Dammit, she'd worked herself into a corner. A dark one, at that.

The only way out was past him. But she had a feeling he wouldn't let her do that.

She lifted her chin high and looked him in the eyes. "Do you know Hernan?"

A flicker of recognition. He flicked his black gaze over her figure, leaving her feeling like a dog had just given her a gross, sloppy kiss.

Resisting the disgusted shudder trying to roll through her, she fought for bravado. It was the only way to get herself out of this dog turd of a mess she'd just stepped squarely in.

"I'm looking for Hernan," she said.

"You one of his women?" The man sneered. Scarier was the fact that he didn't seem to give a damn if she was the "woman" of a man who was powerful and dirty-handed in this town.

"I'm his sister." Maybe that would do the trick.

He cocked a brow and took a step nearer.

Fuck — it hadn't.

Her mouth dried out and she sidestepped him. He followed. She threw a look around. Wasn't anyone going to put a stop to a man's advances on an unwilling woman?

Who was she kidding? These people were out for themselves, and too often lately she'd seen this among all the people who might have once been less ruthless. She threw up a hand to separate him before he got close enough to put his hands on her.

"Lay one hand on me and you'll answer to my brother."

"That so, little beauty?" His Spanish didn't sound like the music it normally did when a man used it to seduce a woman. Right now, she'd take a Cajun drawl any day.

She tried to look for an out without appearing like she was desperate and helpless. There was just enough space under his arm that she might be able to duck and run. She was small and fast.

One song slipped into the next, and she took her chance. She surged forward, dipping under his arm and was just about past him when he snagged her around the middle, swinging her back.

Only he didn't stop there—he walked her three feet away and pinned her to a wall.

Bile rose in her stomach. He smelled of tequila but was still steady on his feet. Either he held his liquor well or hadn't drunk enough to get to the point of toppling over. Too bad — that was exactly what she needed.

Every woman had a few moves to escape a man like this, and Carissa used them, shoving the heels of her hands against his chest hard and rocking him back at the same moment she lifted her knee and rammed him the balls.

He buckled forward on a gasp but then only chuckled and straightened again. What, did he have — balls of steel? She hadn't exactly gone easy on him but maybe she hadn't hit him squarely either.

When he riveted his stare on her, fear hatched and multiplied in her belly. She jerked to the side, but he grabbed her shirt and whipped it upward, exposing her bra.

A roar sounded, and half the patrons around them turned. But Carissa couldn't see what was happening or where the noise was coming from. She could only hope that sound was issued on her behalf.

Bodies were tossed right and left and then a set of shoulders appeared that she recognized *very* well.

Roades' dark eyes zeroed in on her a split second before the man in front of her was lifted and thrown. Then Roades' boot connected in a way that was far more effective than her own knee had been.

Relief left her heart beating too fast and her knees weak. Roades reached out and with one tug had her top back in place.

"You'll answer my questions once I get you outta here." His rough tone brooked no arguments, and she couldn't formulate words that would come out loud enough to be heard over the music and the ruckus of outrage over Roades tossing people around.

He plucked her off her feet and threw her over his shoulder.

Carrying her like a sack of feed out of the club. Laughs sounded behind them all the way to the street and halfway down it, where Roades set her down.

He grabbed her by the shoulders and gave her a once over that was nothing like that other asshole's. It left her feeling warm, safe. Protected.

"You're all right." It wasn't a question—he'd made the assessment with his own two eyes.

She gave a faint nod, her wits quickly returning. "How did you find me anyway? Were you following me?"

"Follow—" He broke off, and she swore she heard his teeth gnash. "Jesus, woman, do you have any idea what could have happened back there? No, I wasn't following you. I happened to be in the right place at the right time, though, don't you think?"

She stared up at him. He'd never spoken to her this way. Then again, this was a new Roades, a harder man who took control and stomped men in the balls hard enough to make them pass out.

He gripped her shoulders harder and shook her a little. "You can't just go out at dark like that. You can't go into places like that. What the hell were you doing?"

"Looking for Hernan." She found her voice and the strength to pull away from him now that her blood was flowing again.

"And did you find him? Fuck, Carissa." He let her go and paced two steps away before whipping back to face her. "You put yourself at risk. Why? Don't you think I can find your piss-ant brother?"

"I..." She couldn't tell him she hoped to handle it herself—to get him to leave sooner so she could start picking up the pieces of her life.

"The US government hires me to handle shit like this, Carissa. The least you can do is show me the same respect and let me do my job. I'm taking you home, and if I have to lock you in there, I will find a way."

"You're really pissed."

He barked a laugh. "You have no idea who you're messing with. When it comes to your safety, I will go to any length to make sure you're all right. If that means dumping bodies in the fucking ocean, I will do it all day and spend the nights scouring the streets for more. Now, do I need to throw you over my shoulder again and carry you home or will you walk?"

She blinked up at him, stunned. The force in which he spoke... about protecting her... It shouldn't have her libido revving but it did. Tendrils of heat dropped low in her belly to make her pussy slick.

He waited, eyes dark and glittering.

"I'll walk," she said quietly.

He took her by the arm and led her back through the streets the way she'd come. She shouldn't be surprised he knew the way as well as she did. Nothing should surprise her anymore when it came to Roades. She wished she knew exactly what dangers he faced. She'd heard stories about the special forces and could only guess, but he was definitely capable of dumping those bodies in the ocean as he'd said.

She didn't know if the power he held frightened her or turned her on. Right now, it was the latter.

All the way back home she reminded herself every hundred steps or so that she wasn't going to fall into bed with him again.

Yet when he took the key from her and unlocked the front door, she watched his hands. So sexy, so capable of brutality or tenderness. For her, it was all tenderness.

He led her inside and made a sweep of the place before firing up an old oil lantern in her bedroom. "Lock the doors. Don't let anybody in. No one followed us—I made certain of that—but that doesn't mean people in that club didn't recognize you and know where to find you. You put yourself on the line just by having the clinic."

"You make that sound like a bad thing — that I help people."

"If it makes you vulnerable, it is." His jaw worked as if biting back something else to say. "Just stay here. Get some rest. You need it."

He did an about-face that would rival the sharpest warrior and left her room. A second later she heard the door shut.

She sat there, considering all that had happened to her in a short time. If she dwelled on what *might* have happened if Roades hadn't shown up at the precise moment she needed him most, she would break out in hives of fear.

Instead, she focused on how he'd stepped in and saved her from being raped, probably in view of everyone in that club too. Each time he battled these people who viewed him as an outsider, he painted a bullseye on his back. Yet he went out into the thick of it again and again, searching for her brother. How soon before he ran Hernan to earth?

She changed from her clothing, feeling grubby after having that man's hands on her. Then slipped on a soft cotton nightgown. Too easily she imagined Roades peeling the cloth up to find her bare skin beneath. Stroking his callused hands over her nipples and pussy until she couldn't think straight.

The sound of the door opening had her bolting out of her bedroom. The only person who could get in was Mari, and she wasn't expected home till morning.

She skidded to a halt on her bare feet to see her brother standing there. He wore clothes that were far too expensive for someone not raking it in by way of other people's desperation.

They stared at each other.

"Heard you were looking for me."

She nodded. "Were you in the club?" Had he been there, watching a man almost rip her top off and done nothing to stop it?

"No, I came in after you left." His face changed as he strode across the room to her. "Why did you call in Roades to hunt me down?"

"I... Hernan, please listen. This isn't you, this life isn't for you. You are so much better than this—"

"No, I'm not, Carissa. That's your mistake to believe that when you've always known different. I'm no good, a criminal. It's in my blood, and I've always known it even if you and our parents fought it."

She blinked at him in disbelief. He couldn't possibly think this—it was the money talking. Some men were easily swayed by riches and changed their personalities once they got their hands on it.

She shook her head. "Hernan, no. The boy I knew—"

"Is the same man you see before you. I know how to get what I want. You can't stop me. And your boyfriend sure as hell can't either."

She studied his eyes and saw a spark of something in the depths—something she recognized as a last glimmer of respect for the man.

She took that information and twisted it. "If you stop, Hernan, I'll send him away. He won't bother you anymore and you never have to face him."

He narrowed his eyes. "You can't do that—send him away. You're in love with him."

She staggered at his words, hurled at her, a blunt fact that felt like blunt trauma. Her chest ached. Yes, she didn't just love the Roades she'd known in her youth, the man she'd wanted to spend the rest of her life with. She loved the Roades she knew now—big, scary secrets, hidden talents and all.

Tears burned at the backs of her eyes. "All right, I love him—I admit it. But for you, I'm willing to throw that away, to send him home. Because you're family, and that's what family does. We have each other's backs. But that means you must stop."

* * * * *

Roades had seen that sneaky fucker working his way back to Carissa's house, and he was going to take care of business here and now.

Except when he silently opened the door and caught Carissa's words, it slammed him hard.

She loved him.

And she was willing to throw that away for family.

144

A noble thing, but it didn't leave Roades feeling all warm and fucking fuzzy.

He edged into the room until he could see Hernan and Carissa, faced off. The kid had filled out over the years and had a cocky stance that made Roades' hands itch to put him in his place.

First, he had to convince Carissa to go in another room and leave him and Hernan to have a *de hombre a homre* talk. He knew she'd never be on board with letting them hash it out man to man, though. She was too stubborn to let him handle it the way he saw fit, even though she'd called him to do it.

Roades braced his legs wide and folded his arms. "Doesn't sound like you're doing well on negotiations," he drawled.

They snapped around to look at him. Hernan's face changed from anger to shock and back again. His eyes drew into slits as he mimicked Roades' pose, folding his arms as well.

Carissa shot a look between them. She moved to step into the middle of it, but Roades gently pushed her back. "We're going to take this discussion outside," he said, holding Hernan's gaze.

The longer Roades looked at him, the more he saw the young kid beneath the strong structure of his face now.

"No." Carissa gave a hard shake of her head. "You're not going outside. Not without me."

They exchanged a look, and at least they had one thing in common—neither wanted Carissa interfering.

She crossed her arms too. So fucking adorable and sassy that Roades had an urge to abandon the whole fight and carry her back to the bedroom.

He jerked his jaw toward the door. Hernan turned and walked out, and Roades followed. Carissa ran to the door, but he looked into her eyes and said, "I promise nothing will happen."

Even if the kid pulled a gun on him, Roades knew how to disarm a man. Hernan might be fully grown but he was no match against Roades.

He quietly closed the door but heard a thump of Carissa hitting the wood on the other side, her ear probably plastered against it. At least she was taking his order to stay inside. If that had been one of his sisters, they'd still be arguing.

"So I hear you've found some free enterprise," Roades drawled out to Hernan.

He rubbed a knuckle over his lip. "I'm no longer fourteen and your words of advice no longer matter to me."

He gave a nod. "That may be so, but I'm still going to try. For Carissa, you understand. Because I love her too."

Hernan continued to stare at him. "She needs to keep her nose out of my business before she gets hurt."

Now threats are a whole other story.

Roades stepped up to the kid. "You will not hurt one hair on your sister's head or have one of your criminal friends do the job. Or you have me to answer to. Understand?"

He snorted. "Like you took care of those guys in the alley. You think you're hurting me, but they mean nothing. They're just stupid kids out to get some cash in their pockets."

"I get it—you're ruthless and untouchable. A big man in this ruined city. But you're not invincible, Hernan. You'll meet your end one day, probably at the hands of somebody you underestimated. Then you'll leave Carissa to deal with the aftermath of collecting and burying your body. Tell me you don't care about that."

"You don't know me."

Roades grunted. "No, but I know your type. I eat your type for breakfast and spit out the bones, little brother. Now listen well. You're going to quit what you're doing, get out of the trading business and find yourself a decent job cleaning up the streets and ruined buildings. No more of this forcing people to pay you for water or food. Got it?"

Hernan laughed.

Roades moved a step closer, using his size to intimidate. "How will you prove to me you're going to quit?"

"Man, it's not all about the money," Hernan scoffed.

"Ah. It's the power. And you used that same power to threaten your sister, didn't you?" His words brought on his own fury, and Roades grabbed Hernan by the shirt front and yanked him in so they were face-to-face. "If you ever fucking threaten her again, I swear to God—"

"Roades, stop!" Carissa's voice rang out, and he realized she'd exited the back of the house and circled to them.

Roades' hands were shaking. If he held onto Hernan another five heartbeats, he couldn't be held accountable for beating him to a pulp. He shoved him away, disgusted and angry that he couldn't do what he wanted to the man.

"Get the fuck outta here before I change my mind about wiping that smug look off your face," he barked.

Hernan threw his sister a look and then vanished into the darkness.

Roades pinched the bridge of his nose, battling to remain in place and not storm after the motherfucker. This hadn't gone the way he hoped—at all. Deep down, he'd known Hernan wouldn't just listen to reason and stop. He was beyond that, but Roades had to try for Carissa's sake. Now he knew Hernan was beyond repair and hope.

Carissa drifted across the grass. "Why did you just let him go?" Her words came out as a whisper.

He dropped his hand and raised his gaze to hers. "For you," he said hoarsely. "To show you what you mean to me and that I'm not the asshole you think I am, incapable of mercy."

A sound broke from her that touched him deep. Then she launched herself into his arms. He caught her against his chest, the softness of her breasts calling to a primal side of him.

She threaded her fingers into his hair. "I'm sorry, Roades."

He leaned in until their foreheads touched. Looking into her glittering dark eyes was the only thing he wanted for the rest of his life. Even now, five years later she was all he could ever dream of having.

"Sorry for what?"

"For believing you don't still have a bit of the man I knew inside you." She went on tiptoe and kissed him. The brush of her lips sweet torture. He stopped breathing for long seconds and when he dragged in a deep breath, her scent overwhelmed him and he lost all grip on his control.

He yanked her against him, body flush. She hooked an ankle around his back, bringing her pussy up against the bulge growing in his pants. They shared a quiet groan and he fumbled a hand under her top to cup the heavy weight of her breast.

Plunging his tongue into her mouth, stroking the fires by clamping his fingertips on her hardened nipple.

She yanked at his waist, finding his belt and managing to unbuckle it and the button of his cargo pants before reality set in. They were standing outside and any neighbors could see them clearly under the light of the moon.

He tore from the kiss, staring down at her beautiful face. "One more time," he rasped out.

"One more time," she agreed.

He lifted her and turned for the house with her in his arms, already feeling the ache of letting her go once the night was through.

Chapter Eight

In the tenseness of Roades' muscles, Carissa felt him holding back. Restraining himself, but why?

"You can't be too rough with me. I won't break," she said between their biting kisses.

He issued a growl but instead of letting go as she'd suggested, he lightened the pressure of his lips.

She bracketed his jaw with her hands and brought him back down again. "I want the real Roades. Show me the man you are now. Teach me."

"Fuck, you don't know what you're asking for, *mon coeur.*"

She slipped her hands over his abs, down to his thick cock, like a rod of steel. She wrapped her fingers around him. "I think I do." With that, she dropped to her knees, tugging down his cargo pants and boxers until his cock sprang free. She leaned in and swallowed it right to the root in one slick move.

"Jesus Christ." He dropped his head back, and she watched his abs dip and shudder with each suck she took. Pulling on him, hollowing her cheeks to gain more suction. Licking the firm head and tasting his precum.

He locked a hand on the back of her head and for the first time, she felt the power behind the man. He yanked her in, forcing her to swallow all of him. A thrill hit her belly and continued lower. Her panties had never been so wet, her nipples so hard. She needed him to give himself up to her for this finale of all time.

She grasped his muscled hips and buried her nose in the fragrant, musky hair at the base of his cock, the head bumping the back of her throat.

He held her there a long second before releasing her and stepping back. His cock bobbed free of her mouth, wet with her saliva, dark purple with need and veins snaking down the length.

She remained on her knees, staring up at him. Then she slowly lifted her hands to pull off her nightgown and cupped her breasts. When she stroked a fingertip over her nipple, he let out a groan. "I need your mouth here, Roades."

He cast off his clothing and in one step was with her, bearing her back on the worn rug of her room and clamping his lips around her nipple. Too tenderly.

Using his ways of doing things, she locked a hand on the back of his head, forcing him down to suck her harder. He did, but it wasn't enough.

"Use your teeth," she whimpered.

"Goddamn, woman, you're going to kill me. Or I'm going to hurt you when I let loose."

She stared into his eyes. "The only way you could hurt me is by not giving your all before you leave me."

She watched the words sink into him one by one until something changed in his eyes. A primitive heat smoldered there, and he bared his teeth before biting down onto her nipple. Not too hard and yet not soft either. The pleasure-pain grounded her in the moment even as she flew on the wings of bliss.

She rocked her hips and he found her wet folds with the tips of his fingers. She expected a gentle brushing over her clit, down to her opening. Instead he thrust them in, high, hard. She cried out and widened her thighs to give him all the access he needed. When he hammered his fingers into her hard and fast, all she could do was hold onto his shoulders and ride the wave of her first orgasm.

It tore through her with a force she'd never known before. This was the Roades she needed now, not the gentle lovemaking of their younger days.

"Fuck me like the man you are now."

He poised at the heat of her, his cock slick with arousal and no barriers between them. She'd take her chances at a pregnancy if this was her one and only time to be with Roades like this.

She wrapped her thighs around him and jerked him into her at the same moment he rocked his hips. Buried so deep she had no idea where their bodies separated.

He slammed his lips over hers, bruisingly. She caught his lip with her teeth and scraped at his shoulders as he pounded into her with a fury of hurricane forces. She took as well as gave, showing him she wasn't the same young girl he'd known and loved but a woman, rock solid and able to withstand anything he threw her way.

Including a life with him.

But he wasn't offering that, only one amazing night, and she was determined to experience every moment.

His biceps quaked, and he churned his hips faster. His kisses left her searing with heat and stole her breath. She jerked upward to take him deeper, and he bottomed out. Again. Again.

The deep knot inside her frayed and suddenly she was pulsating around him, gripping and releasing as she felt the liquid heat of his release pour into her. He threw his head back and roared his pleasure.

Their gazes locked and the lovemaking continued. He pounded into her fiercely and claimed her mouth once more.

This was an end to a chapter of their lives—but no matter how many times she told herself she wasn't falling into his arms again, that he was leaving, she couldn't help but feel it was a beginning too.

* * * * *

"Roades. Everything all right, man?" Ben's voice projected through the phone, and Roades couldn't help but accept how much he missed his brothers. He'd been living, working and playing hard with them for a lifetime.

He considered Ben's question. Everything wasn't exactly all right but shit hadn't gone sideways either.

At least not yet. He still had to force Hernan to stop what he was doing before he could go home. And it wouldn't be done through conversation. Roades would have to apply force of some kind and still keep Carissa on his good side.

"Roades?" Ben prompted.

"I'm here. I need you to pull some strings for me."

"Okaaay. What do you need?"

The plan had been unfolding in his mind since the day he'd set foot on this island. All the things these people needed Roades had free access to. Even their church organization back in Louisiana came to the aid of those in need, and if ever there were people in need, it was here.

As he spilled out the details of getting drop shipments to the deepest parts of the island as well as the cities, and how much money would be needed to rebuild a medical clinic, even a small one, and supply it, Ben just listened.

When he finished, his brother blew out a low whistle. "That's a tall order, Roades. I thought you were asking for transport."

"Shit's complicated here. It's like a war zone."

"Sounds like it."

"Can you get any of what I asked done?"

"I'll try, but you know my time's limited."

Yeah, Knight Ops took over their lives, but it was a small price to pay for what they did to make the world a better place.

"Has Jackson said anything about me coming back?"

"Jackson's being an even bigger asshole than usual. He's got some new woman, and—"

"New woman?"

"Yeah, Dahlia's not handling it very well. It's the first woman he's brought home officially since her mother died."

Ben's wife was a sweetheart and a softie. Roades could see why she'd be affected by her father's new girlfriend.

"You'd think a man would be happier having a woman in his life, not more of an asshole."

Ben chuckled. "Well, he's living his second youth. Last I saw him, he was sporting a five o'clock shadow and riding a Harley."

"Jesus."

"Yeah. I'm guessing he didn't meet this woman at the country club. Anyway, he's nicer, that's true. He's only being an asshole about you."

"Great. Thanks, I feel loads better now." Roades grinned despite the situation. The vision of his superior decked out in leather and unshaven, riding a woman around on the back of his Harley was amusing as hell. The straight-laced, hard-ass he knew would never let stubble sprout on his jaw let alone shirk his friends at the country club.

"Glad to help. But seriously, Roades, I'm not sure I can handle this tall order you've given me."

"Talk to the pastor at least. The church council has funds set up for this type of thing. Go to the mayor too. People rallied for New Orleans after Katrina. They'll want to give back."

"Yeah, you're right. It's just finding the time."

"*Maman* and Lexi could..." He trailed off, realizing the last time they'd spoken it had been about Lexi running off to sow her oats. "Anything about Lexi's whereabouts?"

"She's called home once but we couldn't trace the number. Seems the little shit has learned well from her brothers in the military."

"Fuck. Yeah, it does. Okay, see what you can do. You have a lot of connections, and what you don't have, our parents do."

"I'll run it past Dahlia too. She might know people through her father. Meanwhile, what's going on with you? Did you do what you needed to down there?"

He grunted. "I found the kid, yeah. But I had to let him go."

"Dude, you're losing your touch. A couple months off the team and you can't figure out how to bring in one kid?"

"It's Carissa's brother."

"Shit."

"Yeah. I'd like to wring his goddamn neck, especially since he threatened her. But I have to tread lightly."

"Do you need anything on my end?"

"Not really. I'll handle it." It was just a matter of how much he could piss off Carissa and still be in her good graces. All night long he'd racked his brain for a solution to the not-so-little problem brewing inside him.

He loved her. And he wasn't willing to walk away from a love like that a second time.

Yet he didn't know how to mesh their lives. Her loyalty to her people, especially right now when she was doing so much good with her clinic, would stop her from coming back to Louisiana with him to live. And he couldn't stretch his time between two worlds, his family *and* his team.

No, if it was going to work, sacrifices would need to be made. On whose end was the biggest question and one he couldn't answer.

"You know how to reach me," Ben said and then ended the call.

Roades had been scanning his surroundings during the conversation, but there were no dangers around him. The turmoil was inside him.

He'd been kicking down regrets and slamming back what-ifs all morning. But any way he looked at it, the person making the most sacrifice would be Carissa. He couldn't ask her to leave her life to follow him, even if she felt the same way he did, could he?

Though she'd admitted to Hernan that she loved Roades, that didn't mean she was willing to throw away anything she'd built here. And if she'd been willing to set aside her feelings for Hernan's sake…

Roades sighed and continued walking. At this point, he didn't even know what he was doing here. Searching the streets for what? He was no *policia*, and if he came across Hernan, he wasn't even sure what he'd do now.

Maybe there was something he could do for Carissa, though. Besides get her out of this dangerous town and to a place where she could tend to people without being paid in squashes and apples or dealing in criminal activity with a narcotics trade to get her supplies.

She was a good woman, and he admired everything about what she was sacrificing for the sake of humanity. He also didn't want her anywhere near that sort of life. She deserved a beautiful, comfortable home. A good job in a safe place, but only if she wanted it. If she wanted to stay home and raise their babies, then he would be more than supportive of that.

And after their last encounter, she damn well could be carrying his child.

He had no regrets whatsoever about not using a condom. If she'd turned him away, of course he would have stopped, even wild with need like he was. But when she'd agreed to forego birth control, he'd recognized a feeling of completion and he hadn't even emptied his balls yet.

It was a claiming of sorts, and damn if it wasn't making his dick hard now.

It was time for him to take further action. He wanted her — for life.

Convincing her might be another story. He could tell by the desperation in her last night that she was under the belief that he would soon be walking out on her. Not if he could help it. But his one big fear was that Jackson would lift his probation suddenly, sending him rushing back to meet up with the team. Knight Ops had no choice but to go when called. In the middle of Christmas dinner, birthday parties, lovemaking — didn't matter. They stopped what they were doing and answered the call.

Knowing Carissa like he did, she wouldn't go for that sort of life, though. She liked a quiet life, organization and routine.

He shook his head, unable to drop the weight bearing down on his shoulders when it came to Carissa.

He should be fucking elated that he'd found the woman he wanted to spend his life with, so why was it so damn hard?

* * * * *

Carissa strolled alongside an old friend she'd been in the nursing program with. They chattered about mutual friends and finally got on topic of what her friend had been up to since she no longer had a job.

She waved a hand. "Living like the rest of the island. I hear you're still nursing, though, and I'm happy for you."

"If another clinic ever comes in, will you go back to work?" Carissa asked.

Her friend's eyes were bright. "Yes. I miss it."

A steady drizzle fell on them, but neither cared about the wetness seeping into their hair or the shoulders of their tops. They rounded a corner and Carissa slowed her steps at the sight of the crowd. "What is happening? It's too busy for such a rainy day."

The town square was packed with people, all appeared to be gathered around something.

"Oh, I see my sister." Her friend leaned in to peck Carissa's cheek. "I'll see you soon. Let's not wait so long to get in touch."

Carissa kissed her back and gave her a brief embrace, her attention fixed on the crowd. Shouts were coming back at her, and she made them out.

"Caída de suministro!"

Carissa stopped in her tracks. Supply drop?

She ran up and pushed her way through the bodies until she could see a truck with a huge wooden crate in the back. The driver had his window down, telling them to stand back and form a line so he could distribute the goods. When supplies ran out, another truck was coming and they should wait for it.

Carissa smashed a hand over her thumping heart. After such struggle, she couldn't believe what she was seeing.

Then she really couldn't believe it.

Her heart stuttered as Roades shouldered his way to the truck. The driver caught sight of him and a grin lit his face. He opened the door and jumped down. The pair thumped each other's backs in a man-hug.

Blinking in shock, Carissa was jostled side to side by others trying to get close to the truck. She stood in the middle of the sea, her gaze latched onto Roades.

She hadn't seen him in a few days—he hadn't even slept at her house. And she'd believed it was over between them for good. Now that old love surged upward and fountained out, overflowing in her veins.

She could try to convince herself she didn't need him in her life, but fact was, she *wanted* him. This good man who'd obviously had something to do with a shipment of goods to her island had burrowed into her heart long ago and now he'd taken up every corner there. Evicting him was impossible.

She went on tiptoe, and since he was so tall, she easily made out his profile. He spoke animatedly with the driver.

"Roades!" she called out.

He looked around but didn't immediately set eyes on her. He searched the crowd until she jumped and waved.

He pushed through the crowd and came to her, grabbing her arm and leading her back to the driver. The man was shockingly handsome with a rogue's dark skin and blacker eyes than she'd ever seen, which was saying something with her heritage.

The man let his gaze skip over her face, and something about the intensity sent heat to her cheeks. She introduced herself, and he gave his name, but she missed it as he caught her fingers and brushed his warm lips across them.

His words were also swallowed in the deep, rumbling growl that emerged from Roades.

Roades wrapped an arm around her, yanking her against his side and forcing the man to drop her hand. "This is my fiancée," he said boldly, staring the man in the eyes.

Carissa stifled a gasp. Once, she had been, but no more. Why was he saying this? Just because another man showed obvious interest in her?

"Congratulations to the happy couple, then." The man gave a slow nod of his head out of respect while Roades held onto her, his fingers close to the side of her breast, making her so aware of him it was starting to consume her.

"Thanks again for doing this, *amigo*," Roades said.

Carissa listened for another second, gathering more information from their conversation than anything Roades had said to her in weeks. He'd pulled some strings, gotten more people to rally support and had half a million dollars' worth of food and supplies entering the island.

She tried to hold it back, but the knot in her throat broke free and tears bubbled up and overflowed the rims of her eyes.

The driver noticed and said something to Roades about his fiancée leaking, which made him laugh. He bundled Carissa back through the crowd and some distance away to a ruined wall that once had supported beautiful vines. Now the tropical heat and lack of care had made the vines run rampant and the wall was no longer visible.

Roades took her by the shoulders and looked into her eyes. "Why are you crying?"

"I..." She waved a hand back at the crowd, who was now getting their portions of the shipment. "I can't believe this. How did you do it?" Tears rolled faster.

"Oh *mon coeur*." He palmed the back of her head, drawing her face against his broad, comforting chest. He rubbed her back in little circles that both warmed her and sent tingles of need shooting downward. "Are you upset with me?"

She pushed back to look at his face. "Are you kidding? I'm overwhelmed by your generosity, Roades."

He chuckled. "It's not my money, but I guess if it means you look at me the way you're looking at me, I'll take it."

She slapped at his arm. "How did you do it?"

"A few calls set things into motion." His expression darkened for a second, making her think there was more to the story, but she wasn't going to push right now, when they had so much to discuss.

Namely, him calling her his fiancée.

"Why did you tell that driver we're engaged?"

He stared at her for a long heartbeat and then snapped his mouth shut.

"Roades? Explain."

"You were my fiancée once, and I guess it just slipped out."

She tilted her head. "I'm not buying that. You were jealous of the way he looked at me."

"Hell yeah," he said in a rush of heat as if he'd been holding it back for too long. "He needs to check himself before I do it for him."

"You haven't been back to the house in days."

He rolled with the topic change. "I've been taking care of things."

She arched a brow. "Hernan?"

"Carissa, about Hernan. We need to talk. He can't go on, and you can't expect me to stand by and watch it happen. I know where he's at—I've been keeping an eye on him and… making sure he doesn't leave the area, we'll say."

She almost choked on her tongue. "I don't expect you to do nothing! It's why I called you."

"Yes, but you don't want me to get physical with him, do you?"

"No," she said at once.

"Well, I can't just have a heart-to-heart with the kid anymore. He's unwilling to listen, in case you didn't notice. And the only way to get through a thick skull like that is to…" He broke off.

"To knock him around?"

He shrugged, looking uncomfortable. "Look, I think I have a way worked out to make it stop, but you'll need to trust me and don't ask questions."

Could she do that? He was used to taking charge and only answering to the government for his actions. But this was her brother they were talking about.

He took hold of her shoulders again, looking deep in her eyes. "Carissa, you have to trust me. All right?"

She nodded but she didn't know if she could let things go down and not intervene. She loved them both, wanted the easy route.

She lifted a hand to wipe away the wetness from her eyes. "I need to think for a bit, Roades. I…" She looked back to the crowd, where another truck had rolled up. Her throat tightened again. "Thank you for this."

She turned and started walking, hurrying her footsteps to carry her away from him, to gain distance to think about all that had transpired today. Her emotions were rioting and skipping between the happiness he'd brought to her town to her brother hiding out trying to evade Roades, who was just waiting for her to give him the order to stop Hernan.

All these thoughts kept her on edge—except one. The one where Roades called her his fiancée.

That one melted her heart.

Chapter Nine

First thing Carissa always did after being away from home was check the clinic. Often patients would sit outside on the step and wait for her to return. But this time, someone had walked right inside.

The door hung open, and as she neared, she zeroed in on the lock, which had been forced.

Heart thumping, she stopped in her tracks. Anybody breaking into her clinic would only do so for the drugs she kept there, and that would make them dangerous.

She pressed a palm over her chest to quiet her heart, but it did no good. She listened hard but heard no thumping coming from inside the clinic as someone shifted crates or opened cupboards.

Feeling weak-kneed but determined, she stepped inside.

The place had been ransacked, the contents of the cupboards spilling out onto the floor, many things smashed. One look at the storage closet told her that her entire stash of narcotics had been stolen.

She stumbled back and caught the edge of a counter, gripping it for support. She had nothing left to trade, no way of getting anything she needed and once the supplies she could salvage ran out, her days of treating patients would be finished.

A tear leaked down her cheek, already so close to the surface after what had happened back in the town square with Roades.

She pushed off the counter and flung back the storage room door. Sure enough, the space was empty. Only a roll of gauze lay on the floor, dirty with a boot print.

Hopelessness swallowed her. Despair followed.

She sat down hard on the floor and drew her legs up to her chest, hugging her knees as she looked at the four bare walls. It didn't surprise her that somebody had finally broken in and stolen what she stored here. But the real question rolling around in her mind was who.

Any number of thugs who worked with Angel.

Angel himself.

Or even Hernan.

Her brother would see it as family rights. Anger hit her full force. Her fingers twitched toward the phone she carried. One call to Roades and he'd take necessary steps to stop her brother. But was she ready for that outcome? She couldn't live with herself knowing her brother had been hurt—or worse—at her command.

She rose to her feet and closed the storage room door. The wood hung crookedly on its hinges, and it popped back open, swinging.

She turned away and left the clinic, not bothering to lock the door. If anybody wanted to sort through the destruction there, more power to them.

Maybe it was time to call it quits here in Puerto Rico. She could make a go of it Stateside, and she heard nurses were in high demand there. She could easily find work, get an apartment. Start over.

What was holding her here anyway? Not family. She loved Hernan but would not stand around waiting for someone to kill him for the wrongs he'd done. And she adored Mari, but her cousin had her own life.

Moving to the US would put me closer to Roades too.

Now the tears really flowed.

He was a good man—and the only one she'd wanted then or now. The only obstacle had been his family and their age. Now would they have objections to him marrying her?

She had no answers to the questions burning in her brain, so she made a pot of tea and sat at the table in a ring of sunlight, sipping, and alone with her thoughts.

* * * * *

Roades was pretty damn sick of this town and all the crap it brought with it. He'd like nothing more than to carry Carissa into waiting transport and whisk her out of here. But since he didn't think she'd like it that much, he'd done his best to make her world a better place.

The supplies were a start, and there was more help on the way. But all these things were worthless with people like Hernan on the streets.

Which circled Roades back to his big dilemma — how to handle Hernan and still get the girl.

Because he wasn't giving up on Carissa again. This time, when he left the island, he'd do it with her by his side.

At least he fucking hoped.

His plan was to corner Hernan and lure him into a fight. Only kicking his ass and having enough hurt to break through the haze of bullshit in Hernan's mind would stop him.

At least that had been what Roades thought. Now he wasn't so damn sure.

He ran his fingers through his hair and released a sigh. He should have talked to her about his intentions rather than pushing her to make decisions about how he handled Hernan. Dammit, would he ever stop messing up when it came to Carissa? He fucking loved her, didn't want to go on living without her, yet when was he going to get his shit together and bring it all into one prettily-tied bow?

Looking over the town, one would see bright-colored homes and lush greenery growing rapidly in the tropical heat, overtaking the areas that were no longer inhabited. Just a few weeks on the island had shown Roades differences. The morale had begun to change since his arrival. After losing everything, these people had fought back and were gaining ground by the day. Making headway in the cleanup efforts and finding ways to make life work again.

Areas were already being restored with electric and clean water. When those efforts reached this town, what could Hernan possibly do but stop extorting money from his people? He'd need to move on to some other pursuit.

That was the issue. Hernan would forever be in trouble, it seemed. Roades had heard of it before—people who just couldn't straighten up despite knowing it was morally wrong of them. A deep-seated need for power or money was a driving force, and he suspected the same in Hernan.

Eventually, the guy would end up dead at the hands of somebody he crossed. Or in prison. Either way, Carissa would be left to pick up the pieces of her life and move on without him, just as she had her parents.

Roades had to convince her to come with him. He had money saved, enough for a down-payment for a house. Hell, he could get his *maman* on the job and have a place for them to live by the time they got off this island.

His family would accept her, see nothing to stop them from the love that had kindled long ago. He had to make this happen—he needed to know Carissa was safe and cared for, especially once he was back with Knight Ops.

Again, it circled back to his life's work. Could she handle being the wife of a man like him, as Ben had said on the phone?

When his phone rang, he didn't acknowledge it at first, he was so caught up in the wild beauty of the view and his thoughts. He brought the phone to his ear.

"Roades here."

"Dude, you're back!" His brother, Chaz, practically yelled into his ear.

Roades held his cell out to keep from being deafened and let the words sink in.

"Back?"

"Back on the team. Jackson was looking for you this morning to tell you himself, but he can't find you. Now get your ass back here so we can do some fishin' before the next mission."

"That's great." Why didn't he sound excited? It was all he'd wanted since the moment Jackson put him on probation.

"Need me to send Cohen back to pick you up? We can have you home by tomorrow morning."

"Um. About that. I need some time to wrap up something I've got going here."

"Carissa? Bring her home with you, man. She's welcome. You know our parents don't give a damn who you love now that you're not seventeen."

His chest burned with happiness and yet he had a heavy heart. "It's not Carissa. I've got something to do first. And I'm not sure about Carissa."

"That's cool. You were seeing that old friend from high school—"

He cut Chaz off. "I don't want to date anybody." He wanted to *marry* somebody. He just had some shit to work out before he could think about asking.

"Bachelor it is," Chaz said. His brother was forever a playboy and viewed women as a personal conquest.

"Dude, this isn't about women. I'm doing some good here, and there's something I need to handle before I come back. I hope I'm there in time for the Knight Ops, but if not…"

The line went silent as if Chaz didn't know what to say. Finally, he spoke. "I get it. Well, I don't know what's going on. But I know how it feels to be torn between life and the team. Just know we've got your back, okay?"

The knot in his chest loosened a bit, and he was able to breathe. "Thanks, man. Guts and glory."

"Guts and glory." Chaz rang off, leaving Roades more conflicted than he'd been five minutes before. But it took all of thirty seconds for him to formulate a plan—he'd always been able to think under pressure. He pocketed his phone and turned from the view.

His plan was to take care of Hernan the way Knight Ops had taught him to. The good of the people came first.

Then he was taking care of Carissa. Getting on his knees and begging her to come back to Louisiana with him, if need be. Because she belonged with him.

His strides were long as he set off into the barrio where he knew Hernan had been hiding. The slum area was one of the worst Roades had seen, and it practically reeked of desperation.

Well, he'd do his best to help anybody he came across, unless it was Carissa's brother. Then the kid was having a coming-to-Jesus moment.

"Oye, senor!"

He turned at the child's voice. Sitting on a curb was a little boy with a scrappy-looking dog next to him. The dog had a chew mark on its ear, as if it'd been in a recent fight. The boy was just as skinny with bruises on his shins.

Roades approached them slowly, so as not to frighten them. He spoke to the boy softly in his native tongue, learning the dog's name and if the child was going to school. He wasn't, which didn't surprise Roades but saddened him. The kid looked to be bearing the weight of the world on his shoulders, when he should be out riding his bike and playing stickball with friends.

Hooking a thumb in the pocket of his cargo pants, Roades settled in for a longer chat.

Something whizzed by his head that was all too familiar to a Marine.

He hit the dirt, catching the boy and the dog in the process and rolling them backward against a building. Trapping them with his body, he whipped out his sidearm and aimed in the direction the bullets had come from.

Another bullet smacked off the building next to his head. He had to get this kid the fuck out of here.

Throwing a look back over his shoulder, he ordered, "Scoot into those shadows between buildings, get down and cover your head. Now!"

But the kid nonchalantly wiggled out from behind Roades and sauntered into the nearby house with his dog on his heels.

Roades stared at him for a heavy heartbeat. Jesus, someone had probably paid the kid to lure passersby into conversation so they could rob him.

Roades rolled to his feet in a blink, weapon at the ready. "Show your face!"

Two guys rounded a building and stepped into the street across from where Roades stood. One still bore the bruises on his face that Roades had put there himself back in that alley, one of the men Carissa had seen him use his martial arts on in his first hours on the island.

"Didn't get enough?" Roades' drawl was nothing but casual, and he aimed at the man pointing a gun at him.

The man grunted and opened his mouth to speak, but his gaze darted to the side.

Roades twitched a glance sideways to see Hernan standing feet away from him.

And Carissa's brother had Roades in *his* sights.

"Y'all working together?" Roades would admit he was starting to sweat. He could smell it on himself, that sour scent of adrenaline.

"Fuck no. We hate this *hijo de puta*," one of the men across the street yelled. Roades detected the shift of the man's shoulder before he squeezed off the shot.

The force of the bullet threw Hernan back, and Roades aimed and fired, taking out the shooter just as another shot rang out—from Hernan.

The bullet grazed Roades' shoulder, searing it with pain. At first he thought Roades had fired out of reflex of being shot, but the grin on the kid's face was anything but friendly.

"Hold still so I can shoot your fucking ass," Hernan said.

Roades knocked the weapon from his hand and assessed the damage done to Carissa's brother—gut shot with the rich blood of a lacerated liver. It was a wonder the man was still drawing breath. He'd bleed out quickly if he didn't get medical help now.

Two more men emerged onto the street, and Roades took in the situation in a blink.

There were far too many men who wanted him off the island, preferably dumped into the ocean. But he had to get Hernan to aid.

A scuffing sound met his ears and he shot a look from the corner of his eye to see Hernan crawling across the cracked pavement toward his weapon.

Roades kicked it out of the way. "Stay still. I'll get you to a hospital."

"Gonna... get rid of you. First." Hernan grinned around bloody teeth.

"Goddammit." Roades' mutter was lost on a battle cry from the gang on the street. They rushed Roades, and he had two writhing on the ground with bullets buried deep in the shoulders of their shooting arms.

With seconds to spare, Roades snatched up Hernan's weapon and then dragged the man up and over his shoulder. Hot blood trickled through Roades' clothes.

"You need to... get the fuck out." Hernan's voice gurgled.

Nicked a lung maybe. Jesus, Roades was trained to know how to give a syrette of morphine or when to apply a tourniquet, but neither of those treatments would apply here. He needed a hospital, but it was fucking unlikely he'd find anybody in this godforsaken barrio and the clinic in town had closed.

That left only Carissa.

178

Another shot rang out just as Roades cornered a building, running full-out.

He'd go back and finish the fight if he ever got a chance, but for now he was going to try to save the asshole who'd tried to kill him.

"You're a dick, you know that?" he bit off to Hernan.

A wheeze came from over his shoulder, maybe a laugh.

"Imagine. Those guys wanted both you and me dead. And you were trying to kill me too. I shoulda shot all of ya and left you to the stray dogs for dinner." Roades was enraged at the situation and the furrow in his arm was screaming in pain, but he'd had worse. His biggest concern was dropping Carissa's half-dead brother in her clinic.

The barrio was a blur as he booked it as fast as he could. The buildings that were slumping and weathered began to look slightly less slumping and weathered. He spotted some men gathered on a corner and called out to them.

"Doctor?"

They shook their heads and turned away, not wanting to get involved in whatever crisis Roades was dealing with.

Fuck, what he wouldn't do to go back and finish that fight. The need to sink his fists into bodies and make sure those guys never touched weapons again...

He dammed up that stream of thought and focused on Hernan's breathing. In, out. Rattle. In, out, rattle. Definitely a nicked lung, which would account for the blood on his teeth. When he'd lifted the kid, Roades had felt the exit wound on his back. He should have placed a wet cloth over it to do his best to stop the sucking wound. But it had been life or death so he'd taken the only option he could — to run and save them both.

Did he have time to lower Hernan to the ground and do that now?

No, he was within half a mile of Carissa's house, and getting Hernan there was more important.

He hadn't carried a man out of battle in a long time, and his thighs were burning with effort.

Oh fuck, it was just one thigh.

Still holding his weapon, he dropped his arm and ran his thumb over the spot that hurt the most.

Jesus, he was hit there too. How the fuck had he managed to ignore that?

Doesn't matter.

He skidded around a corner, taking a shortcut to Carissa's. Now that the pain had hit him, it came on with a vengeance and his own breathing was ragged as he reached the garden.

"Carissa!" he bellowed.

The clinic door was open and he burst inside, not fully understanding what he was seeing.

180

The place was wrecked. Supplies lay all over the floor, every cupboard ripped apart and the doors off their hinges in some cases.

He spotted the cot, though, and lay Hernan down as gently as he could, though the kid grunted in pain.

A step at the door brought Roades' head up and he stared into Carissa's eyes.

"Oh my God." Her voice faltered.

He strode to her and grabbed her shoulders. "He's been shot. Tell me what to do."

Her gaze slid past him to her brother lying on the cot, his face ashen and blood spilling from his lips. "Did you do this?"

"Hell no. Carissa, listen to me. We need to help him. Tell me what to do."

She gave a wobbly nod and walked over to the cot. She placed a hand on Hernan's chest and looked into his eyes. Then she raised her hand to cup Hernan's cheek. "Hail Mary full of grace..."

The prayer came off her lips in a slow Spanish that had Roades baffled.

He strode to the cot, realizing he was limping and his thigh wasn't supporting his weight. He leaned hard on the side of the bed. "What the hell are you doing? He needs help, not prayers!"

"Prayers are all I can do for him right now. He needs emergency surgery and we'll never get him to someone in time." She sounded eerily calm, and Roades knew she was in shock.

He gripped her hand and Hernan's too, finishing the prayer with her.

"S-s-sorry," Hernan choked out.

The word seemed to bring Carissa out of her own hazy mind. "I love you, brother. No matter what, I forgive you." She leaned in and kissed her brother between the brows before turning to Roades. "I can't do more for him, but I can help you now. You're covered in blood and it isn't all his. Where are you hit?"

He considered her for a moment. This was wrong any angle he looked at it, but Carissa was trained to triage patients, and it was his turn.

His thigh was burning like a motherfucker now, and he pointed to the spot that had the most damage. But he glanced back to Hernan. "Can't you do more for him, Carissa?"

She shook her head, her lips taking on a grave expression, and pushed on Roades' chest until he sat in a chair. At her feet were bundles of gauze and some toweling, and she swiped the supplies off the floor.

"I can't treat you with these. They're not sterile."

"Better'n nothing." He grabbed a towel from her hand and pressed it hard against his leg.

A gurgling noise rose from the cot, and Roades got to his feet. Carissa went back to her brother, looking down at him with love written on her beautiful face as he drew his last breath.

* * * * *

She couldn't look at Roades after her brother died. She believed when he said he hadn't done it, but what had he been doing with Hernan in the first place?

She gently patted her brother's limp hand and placed it on the cot next to his thigh. Then she grabbed a sheet and covered him to the neck. She hesitated, wondering if she should continue up over his face but unable to in the end.

Turning back to Roades, she pointed to the chair.

He took the seat, his gaze intense on her face, but she still couldn't look him in the eyes. Tears had never felt so far from the surface. They were buried too deep, and that ache of loss—for her brother, for Roades when he inevitably went home—was too wide.

She stuck two fingers into the tear in his cargo pants and ripped the fabric. With a gaping bullet wound exposed, she rocked back on her heels.

"Carissa," he said, snapping her out of whatever daze had swallowed her.

She stared at a point on his square jaw, dark with stubble and spots of blood that might or might not belong to him.

"What supplies do you need to stop this bleeding?" he asked.

That set her in motion. She moved away from him and started searching through cupboards and drawers. When she found some items in the packaging, sterile and ready to go, she tore into the paper.

"The bullet needs to come out."

"Have you ever done that before?" he asked, a bit too gently. Tears rose in her eyes, and she blinked through them.

She shook her head. "I can only stop the bleeding. I'm not trained to perform the surgery."

He reached across his body and touched his pocket. "My cell. Get it for me."

Reaching into his pocket, touching the hard muscle that she'd spent many hours stroking and latching on to as he pleasured her, was surreal. She felt as if she was floating outside of her body, unable to find the ground again.

She worked the cell free and placed it in his hand. He took it and punched a button then brought it to his ear. Using the thumb and forefinger of his free hand, he pinched her chin and lifted her face.

She couldn't meet his gaze, didn't want to see the things he'd done reflected in his eyes. Didn't want him to see the pain that must be shining in hers.

"*Mon coeur* – " He broke off as whoever answered on the other end of the line. "Ben, I need airlift. Now."

He gave the details in short bursts of speech. When he ended the call, he let go of her chin and smoothed his hand through her hair. The caress brought another round of tears to her eyes and one let loose, dropping when she bowed her head.

184

"I'm so goddamn sorry about your brother," he grated out.

Her tears fell faster, and she drew back from his touch. "I'd... like you to tell me what happened when we're done here."

She'd lost a brother today. But she was losing the love of her life as well.

"I'll tell you anything you need to know, *mon coeur.*"

She moved through the clinic, gathering what she could to keep his wounds stable for transport. Flying back to the States with a bullet in his thigh wasn't ideal, but if she attempted to pull it out, arteries would need ligated and she didn't have the means or training to do such a thing.

She threw a glance at the white sheet dangling off the side of the cot where Hernan lay but quickly averted her gaze. She wanted to run from this life and hide. It was too damn hard now, and she had nothing left here for her.

Especially after Roades was gone.

Chapter Ten

Christ, she couldn't even meet his gaze, and it was fucking killing him. Through the recounting of the story and calling someone to take care of Hernan, as Roades grabbed his duffel and awaited transport, Carissa hadn't looked into his eyes one time.

She leaned against the cot, now empty since Hernan had been carried away for burial preparations. She looked so damn lost, so alone. And she fucking *was* alone once he left this godforsaken place.

"I pray your leg isn't septic by the time you reach home," she said for the second time.

He shook his head. "I've got people coming to take care of it in flight if necessary."

Her gaze shot upward but didn't quite meet his. He was going nuts by now, desperate to make her engage with him, even if it was to tell him off, pound her fists against his chest or scream until she collapsed, hoarse.

He ran his hand through his hair and fought his rising panic. In minutes, somebody would arrive to transport him to the nearest landing strip.

"I'm sorry, Carissa. So damn sorry for all of it."

Her throat worked but she only nodded, as distant as she ever could be. His hopes and dreams of asking her to marry him, of taking her home and buying that house... they all swept away on a wave of grief and pain.

A deep hollow opened inside him, and it was all too easy to fall in head first.

The rumble of an engine outside got him to his feet. She pulled away from the cot and stood before him, eyes downcast.

His bruised heart cracked open and bled out faster than his leg ever could. He lifted a hand to her jaw. "God, you're so damn beautiful."

A noise left her that wasn't quite a sob. She placed her hand over his. "Godspeed, Roades."

"Take care of yourself." He let her go and walked out before he broke the fuck down. Dammit, leaving her once had almost killed him, and he'd only been a kid then. Now walking away was a thousand times worse. She was linked to him, her soul bound to his in a way that would never, ever happen again. She was it.

He greeted his fellow Marine and climbed into the vehicle. All the way to the airstrip, he listened to the guy talk about the efforts they were employing on the island to clean up and keep peace. He wanted more details about Roades' wound, but he remained silent, unwilling to speak about what happened and too deep in his thoughts to even find words.

The bumpy road didn't help the pain he was experiencing, but he gritted his teeth through it like any good Marine would. His phone buzzed several times, and he took calls from two of his brothers regarding timeframes and surgeons on standby awaiting his arrival. He got through it but barely, though his heart was ripped out, back in Carissa's hands.

The driver came to a stop and Roades got out, aware of shooting pains through his thigh as he made his way across the broken concrete to the small government-issue jet that often carried generals and officials through the skies.

He turned to shake his driver's hand. "Thank you."

"An honor." He saluted Roades, and a knot burned in his throat. Roades loved his country and serving with Knight Ops. Now just as he was reinstated he'd be off on medical leave, recovering from this leg injury.

None of that mattered.

He shouldered his duffel, wincing at the strain on the bullet furrow across the other, and made his way to the jet.

There, the pilot and copilot greeted him, along with two medical personnel who'd been ordered to see him safely home.

"You don't look like a man with a bullet in your thigh," one commented with a grin.

"I'm made of tougher stuff than most. I'm a Knight." He reached up to take the edge of the door and climb the steps when a loud horn blast made him jerk around.

An old truck was speeding across the airstrip toward them. It screeched to a stop and Roades searched the windshield. The faces behind it were of an older man he didn't recognize and a woman.

A flurry of activity from inside and he could swear the woman kissed the older man on the cheek before leaping out of the truck.

Roades' heart stopped.

"Carissa." Her name passed his lips on a harsh groan.

He dropped his duffel and started for her as she sped toward him, running as fast as a track star.

He opened his arms and she slammed into his chest. He wrapped his arms around her, holding her tight so she'd never get away from him again.

"I'm sorry, Roades! I love you so much and it kills me to think of you leaving. That's why I was so stubborn back there, barely saying goodbye to you." She lifted her head and met his gaze at long last.

Her dark eyes burned through him, and he let out a rough sigh of relief.

She loved him.

He crushed his lips down on hers, tasting her tears and the sweetness that meant he'd come home.

Angling his head, he swept his tongue through her mouth and pulled a moan from her. She kissed back with a fervor that instantly had him thinking of how to fuck her even with a bullet in his leg.

"I love you, Roades. So much."

He drew away to look into her eyes. She didn't even try to look away. "Get on this plane with me. Come home. And marry me."

* * * * *

She'd only thought to find him and say a proper goodbye, but now that he was asking her for more, her heart leaped into her throat.

Could she do that? Walk away from her home, from her life?

Now that Hernan was gone, what else did she have? She could return to visit her cousin or invite her to Louisiana.

But... marriage? She'd be the wife of a man whose first commitment was to his country, and that meant he'd be gone a lot. He'd also have secrets he couldn't share with her, about where he'd been and what he'd done.

All this ran through her mind in a heartbeat.

"Roades," she whispered.

"I'd drop to one knee and ask properly, *mon coeur*, but this thigh hurts like hell."

She gripped his arm hard. "Don't you dare, Roades Knight!"

"Come with me. Keep my mind from the pain during the flight and we'll lay out our plans."

Her eyes scalded with tears. "Hernan is to be buried."

"I can make sure that doesn't happen until we come back after my surgery."

"No, no. You need to recover. I..." She didn't want to stay behind while he walked this path alone. She wanted to kiss him before he went into the OR and be there when he opened his eyes afterward, as well as each step of recovery he took.

"My brother. We'll have him cremated and I'll come back for his ashes."

Roades' stare intensified. "Does this mean you're coming with me?"

She spread her hands. "I have nothing. No clothes."

"Don't worry — *Maman* loves to shop."

Her heart tripped and then tumbled. "My patients..."

She turned to look at the truck where Mr. Báez still sat, waiting for her to return with him. She'd never considered this was a one-way trip when asking him for help.

"We'll do more from the States, rally more support. Rebuild Puerto Rico. But it isn't safe here, and I can't let you remain without me."

191

She turned and looked at the truck she'd arrived in. Did she want to walk away from everything? Roades was right, more could be done with the right people to help. Here, she was working alone.

And would *be* so alone.

She lifted her hand and waved goodbye to Mr. Báez. He waved back and slowly reversed the truck.

She spun back to Roades, and the expression of joy on his face was something she wanted to see there every day for the rest of her life.

"Let's get you to that hospital." She took charge, looking to the medical personnel watching the scene. She pointed to one. "He needs painkillers." She spouted off a dosage. "And he's been walking on that leg. We need to make sure it's stabilized. I'm not sure where that bullet is, and if it slips —"

One laid a hand on her shoulder. "He'll be in good hands, we promise. Welcome aboard." He helped her into the jet, and she waited there until Roades made his way up the steps too. She fussed over him until he was settled.

He hooked an arm around her middle and yanked her forward to crush his lips over hers. "As happy as I am that you agreed to come with me, you haven't given me an answer about my proposal."

What a horrible and wonderful day this was, and her emotions were twisted up. But she disentangled them long enough to clasp his face in her hands.

Looking deep into his eyes, she leaned in until their foreheads touched.

"I love you, Roades. And while I don't claim to understand your life or your job, I am willing to learn it all. Because I want to be with you."

The kiss they shared was sweet, lingering.

Epilogue

Louisiana bayous were a different world from what Carissa was accustomed to, but the same sun hung overhead as it did all over the world. She stretched out on her stomach, letting the rays heat her skin and make her even sleepier than she already was.

She yawned, and Roades chuckled. "You didn't get much rest last night," he said.

She cracked an eye to look at his profile, where he lay next to her on the blanket they shared. The water of the bayou lapped against the dock supports, and out here at the Knight family's cabin, it was the quietest, most peaceful place on earth.

A perfect honeymoon spot.

"It isn't like you feel bad about keeping me awake," she teased with a flick of her brow that meant she wouldn't care if he tried it again.

He laughed and rolled onto his side to take her in his arms. "I plan to bring you here every year and do this very thing, Mrs. Knight, *mon coeur.*"

Her new status made her warm from the inside out. She slung a bare thigh across his waist, aware of his thigh injury. Though healing well, it still gave him some pain especially after exertion or at night.

She ran a hand down his chest to his midsection, using her fingertips to tease the muscled ridges there. "We need *some* rest. We fly out for Puerto Rico in two days."

"That's true. We need to be prepared to work hard."

Three weeks on the island would do a lot of good for the people. Their plans extended from medical facilities to youth shelters and so much more. She didn't know if three weeks would even be enough, but after that, Roades should be cleared to return to Knight Ops.

They'd spoken extensively about what she should expect. He'd even told her about a few missions, though she suspected he'd only shared the simple, safest ones.

"I might have an obligation for us tomorrow as well. Or my family does."

She leaned onto an elbow, hovering over him, her long hair draped around his face and sheltering them both from the baking sun. "What didn't you tell me?"

"After the wedding, my family told me to hurry back from the cabin because they have a reception planned for us."

"A party?"

He nodded. "Friends and family only, though that is large enough, especially now that Lexi's home from her adventures. I just wish Tyler was on leave to join us."

"I haven't seen her since she was so young. Is she much changed?" Carissa asked.

He barked a laugh. "Do you remember her as a hellion?"

She nodded.

"Then she hasn't changed. Now, enough talk. More kissin'." He drew her atop him, and she rubbed her pussy against his erection that was already solid and ready for her to sink over.

"It's only a matter of time before I'm pregnant, you know." He'd refused to let them use any birth control since that one night they'd gone without.

A smile split his rugged, handsome features. "Let's hope so. I want some sons."

"And daughters?" She smacked at him.

He caught her hand and drew her knuckles to his lips. The heat of his mouth over her skin sent liquid heat down between her legs. She eased over the tip of his cock and began a slow descent meant to torment her husband.

"And daughters," he said on a groan as she fully seated herself over him and began to ride.

The words fell away, leaving only the music of their lovemaking and the sounds of the bayou of Carissa's new home.

READ ON FOR A SNEAK PEEK OF THE NEXT BOOK IN THE KNIGHT OPS SERIES, KNIGHT SHIFT

Fleur dropped to her knees in front of the motel bathtub and doused her head in the hot water pouring from the tap. Her hands shook as she ran her fingers through her dark brown locks, now bleached blonde.

She'd never touched her hair with bleach or dye before now, and the outcome would be far from perfect, but the trashier she looked, the harder she'd be to find. She had to get out of here.

Frankie's dying word, rough and burbling from the gunshot he'd suffered, had been: "Run." And she was.

She squeezed out her length of hair and grabbed a towel. Wetness trickled down her nape to dampen her top, but she ignored it as she frantically dried her hair. She didn't have long before they located her.

The events jumbled in her mind. Being called to Frankie's small bungalow outside of New Orleans. How he'd dropped the call without saying goodbye. That was her first clue something was wrong.

Frankie's house wasn't a place she visited often, but the suburb felt like home each time she drove through the quiet, quaint, historical district, but even the shadows cast by the older trees had seemed ominous.

She gulped down her rising emotions.

She loved Frankie. Her father's friend had been in her life... well, forever.

And now he was dead.

She yanked the towel away and twisted to stare into the foggy motel mirror. Her thick dark hair was now a buttery blonde. Not as flattering as her real color but not horrible.

She still looked like Fleur Sutton, though. That had to change.

Digging in the bag of items she'd purchased on a mad dash through the drugstore, she came out with a pair of scissors. The most she'd ever done was give her own bangs a trim or cut off some split ends, but she lifted the shears to her head. How bad could it turn out?

She yanked out a hank of hair and set the scissor blades on it. To completely change her appearance, she should go short.

But in the end, she slid the blades farther down the lock and started cutting just below her shoulders. Bit by bit the blonde strands dropped into the sink and she looked less and less like Fleur Sutton.

She'd need a new name along with a fake ID. A few of her father's friends would know where to get one, but she had to steer clear of them. Each and every one was loyal to her father in ways she'd never questioned until this afternoon.

When she'd turned up at Frankie's house, he'd been tossing clothes into a duffel and barking information at her. He had to leave the city, now. Would never see her or get in touch with her again. If she was smart, she'd leave too but not before she found a certain man by the name of Antonio and asked him to give her the bag.

She ducked her head, replaying the scene behind closed eyes...

What's in the bag? she'd asked, panic rising.

He'd tossed a look her way, a slice that cut deep and left an icy coldness she didn't understand and hadn't even begun to process now.

I don't know what's in the bag, Fleur. But it has to do with you. Your father gave it to me for safekeeping.

You never looked?

No. You know I can't cross your father.

At that moment, she'd seen movement outside — a car pulling up. A car she recognized. Relief swam through her — her father's friend would help Frankie with whatever was wrong. She started to the door, but Frankie grabbed her back.

Hide yourself and don't come out no matter what you hear.

But Raymond will see my car and know I'm here.

Dammit, you shouldn't have parked out front!

Frankie had frantically worked bullets into a handgun while Fleur looked on, shocked.

Raymond isn't going to hurt us.

You sure about that?

A second later, her father's friend had stormed into the house without knocking, circling through the rooms and calling for Frankie in a taunting voice. When he got to the bedroom where he and Fleur stood, his gaze slid to her.

Get out, Fleur. This doesn't have anything to do with you.

Terror had her blood running cold. Was Raymond, a man she liked and trusted, going to shoot Frankie in cold blood?

What are you doing, Raymond? This is my father's friend.

Not anymore. No room for friends who betray, who sing when a little pressure's put on them.

She looked between them. Frankie held the weapon out, pointed at Raymond's chest. Raymond's pistol was trained on Frankie's. If she didn't do something to stop this, they'd both end up dead.

She stepped up, heart tripping wildly. *Don't do this. Let's talk.*

Too much talk going on, isn't that right, Frankie? You're good at spilling secrets. Fleur, this is my last warning to leave. You don't need to be around when this happens.

When this happened? Oh God.

She racked her brain and an idea formed. She lifted her jaw a notch, looked into Raymond's eyes

200

and lied straight to his face. *My father wants to question him further. He told me.*

Raymond's gaze turned to her, contemplation there. *You talked to your father about this?*

Yeah, he… She stumbled mentally but recovered quickly. *He told me to set Frankie straight myself. Why do you think I'm here?*

You're working with your father now? On this side of operations?

Was there another side to operations on the plantation?

Frankie looked at her, horror on his face. She couldn't ease his mind, couldn't tell him she was faking her way through to save what seemed to be his life right now.

Yeah, and he told me to bring Frankie to him. She put her hand on the man's arm, applying the slightest pressure she hoped Raymond didn't notice and Frankie understood as friendship. *Come on, Frankie. I'll drive you.*

Before she was able to get him to take a single step, Frankie squeezed off a shot. The bullet went wild, ricocheting off a bedpost and missing Raymond.

But Raymond's shot was true.

Frankie had crumpled. And life as she knew it faded to black.

In the mirror, tears burned in her eyes, far too dark brown to be anything but the French Creole that her mother had passed down to her.

She'd need to get some non-prescription, colored contacts at a costume store and fast.

But with what money? She'd fled with only a few bucks in her pocket, only enough for dye, scissors, a black hoodie with a rock band logo on it and a motel room. She had all of ten bucks left—enough for a fast food meal. Luckily her gas tank was full, and she could drive for hours. What then? As soon as she used her bank or credit cards, her father would be able to track her movements. The last person she wanted to find her right now was her father.

Hands shaking, she finished off her haircut and lowered the scissors. Her mind was shocked into a reality she did not want to face. All she wanted to do was go home, and that was the last place she could ever set foot again.

Not knowing what was happening after seeing her father's friend kill Frankie, she'd driven straight to the family's plantation. But when she'd neared her father's office door, she'd overheard a conversation with Raymond's brother.

"It's done."

"Good." She heard the telltale squeak of her father's chair and knew he was leaning back, hands templed in thought, rocking.

"I didn't know you were sending Fleur to talk to Frankie before I got there. Good to bring her into the family business at last, though, right?"

The squeaking stopped, and her heartrate jumped to a rate so high, dizziness swept her.

"Fleur. My Fleur."

"Yes, sir. She said you sent her because you wanted to question Frankie further."

"Family business… There isn't room for Fleur in the family business. Especially after what she's seen."

Her blood ran cold at the chilling threat.

Silence and then: "Bring her in."

She still didn't know how she'd gotten her legs to actually work, to run out of the house and not be detected, though Daddy would see it eventually on the security camera footage.

None of this made sense. Her father had ordered a hit on her friend—on his own friend. And she wasn't sticking around to find out what her father would do with her.

Her tears fell in earnest, and she swiped them off her cheeks. Staring at her new reflection, she said, "Shoot, shovel and shut the fuck up." That had been a motto she'd heard far too many times in her lifetime growing up, and now the words had a far different meaning than what she'd always assumed.

With crop damage from marauding deer and who knew what else a constant problem, it seemed logical that her father and his men wouldn't think twice about taking game out of season. But now...

She had to get the hell out of here—fast. She took the bag from the drugstore and dumped the bleach and all her newly cut hair into it. She tied it shut and walked out, leaving the key locked inside the room, and tossed the bag into the dumpster on the way to her car.

As she climbed behind the wheel, Frankie's smiling face loomed in her memory. It was all she had now to carry with her of the man who'd been like a second father to her.

Her heart pumped hard and she tried to draw in deep, measured breaths. She didn't want to pass out behind the wheel.

Driving in New Orleans was too conspicuous. Anybody who knew her father would easily pick out her sleek black luxury car given to her on her twenty-first birthday.

She'd have to ditch it somewhere and get a rental.

Again, with what money?

Who could she trust to help her? Only Frankie came to mind.

Can't think about that now. She needed cash, contacts, a new ID and another car.

Or maybe not.

She drove into the heart of a bad neighborhood, one under constant spotlight on the evening news. Parking along the curb in broad daylight didn't cause anyone to even look her way. Not even when she got out and started walking. She left the keys in it and didn't look back.

1-click KNIGHT SHIFT

Em Petrova

Em Petrova was raised by hippies in the wilds of Pennsylvania but told her parents at the age of four she wanted to be a gypsy when she grew up. She has a soft spot for babies, puppies and 90s Grunge music and believes in Bigfoot and aliens. She started writing at the age of twelve and prides herself on making her characters larger than life and her sex scenes hotter than hot.

She burst into the world of publishing in 2010 after having five beautiful bambinos and figuring they were old enough to get their own snacks while she pounds away at the keys. In her not-so-spare time, she is fur-mommy to a Labradoodle named Daisy Hasselhoff.

Find More Books by Em Petrova at empetrova.com

Other Titles by Em Petrova

West Protection
HIGH-STAKES COWBOY
RESCUED BY THE COWBOY

GUARDED BY THE COWBOY
COWBOY CONSPIRACY THEORY
COWBOY IN THE CORSSHAIRS
PROTECTED BY THE COWBOY

Xtreme Ops
HITTING XTREMES
TO THE XTREME
XTREME BEHAVIOR
XTREME AFFAIRS
XTREME MEASURES
XTREME PRESSURE
XTREME LIMITS
Xtreme Ops Alaska Search and Rescue
NORTH OF LOVE

Crossroads
BAD IN BOOTS
CONFIDENT IN CHAPS
COCKY IN A COWBOY HAT
SAVAGE IN A STETSON
SHOW-OFF IN SPURS

Dark Falcons MC
DIXON

TANK
PATRIOT
DIESEL
BLADE

The Guard
HIS TO SHELTER
HIS TO DEFEND
HIS TO PROTECT

Moon Ranch
TOUGH AND TAMED
SCREWED AND SATISFIED
CHISELED AND CLAIMED

Ranger Ops
AT CLOSE RANGE
WITHIN RANGE
POINT BLANK RANGE
RANGE OF MOTION
TARGET IN RANGE
OUT OF RANGE

Knight Ops Series
ALL KNIGHTER
HEAT OF THE KNIGHT

HOT LOUISIANA KNIGHT
AFTER MIDKNIGHT
KNIGHT SHIFT
ANGEL OF THE KNIGHT
O CHRISTMAS KNIGHT

Wild West Series
SOMETHING ABOUT A LAWMAN
SOMETHING ABOUT A SHERIFF
SOMETHING ABOUT A BOUNTY HUNTER
SOMETHING ABOUT A MOUNTAIN MAN

Operation Cowboy Series
KICKIN' UP DUST
SPURS AND SURRENDER

The Boot Knockers Ranch Series
PUSHIN' BUTTONS
BODY LANGUAGE
REINING MEN
ROPIN' HEARTS
ROPE BURN
COWBOY NOT INCLUDED
COWBOY BY CANDLELIGHT
THE BOOT KNOCKER'S BABY
ROPIN' A ROMEO

WINNING WYOMING

Ménage à Trouble Series
WRANGLED UP
UP FOR GRABS
HOOKING UP
ALL WOUND UP
DOUBLED UP novella duet
UP CLOSE
WARMED UP

Another Shot at Love Series
GRIFFIN
BRANT
AXEL

Rope 'n Ride Series
BUCK
RYDER
RIDGE
WEST
LANE
WYNONNA

The Dalton Boys
COWBOY CRAZY Hank's story

COWBOY BARGAIN Cash's story
COWBOY CRUSHIN' Witt's story
COWBOY SECRET Beck's story
COWBOY RUSH Kade's Story
COWBOY MISTLETOE a Christmas novella
COWBOY FLIRTATION Ford's story
COWBOY TEMPTATION Easton's story
COWBOY SURPRISE Justus's story
COWGIRL DREAMER Gracie's story
COWGIRL MIRACLE Jessamine's story
COWGIRL HEART Kezziah's story

Single Titles and Boxes
THE BOOT KNOCKERS RANCH BOX SET
THE DALTON BOYS BOX SET
SINFUL HEARTS
JINGLE BOOTS
A COWBOY FOR CHRISTMAS
FULL RIDE

Club Ties Series
LOVE TIES
HEART TIES
MARKED AS HIS
SOUL TIES
ACE'S WILD

EM PETROVA
WWW.EMPETROVA.COM